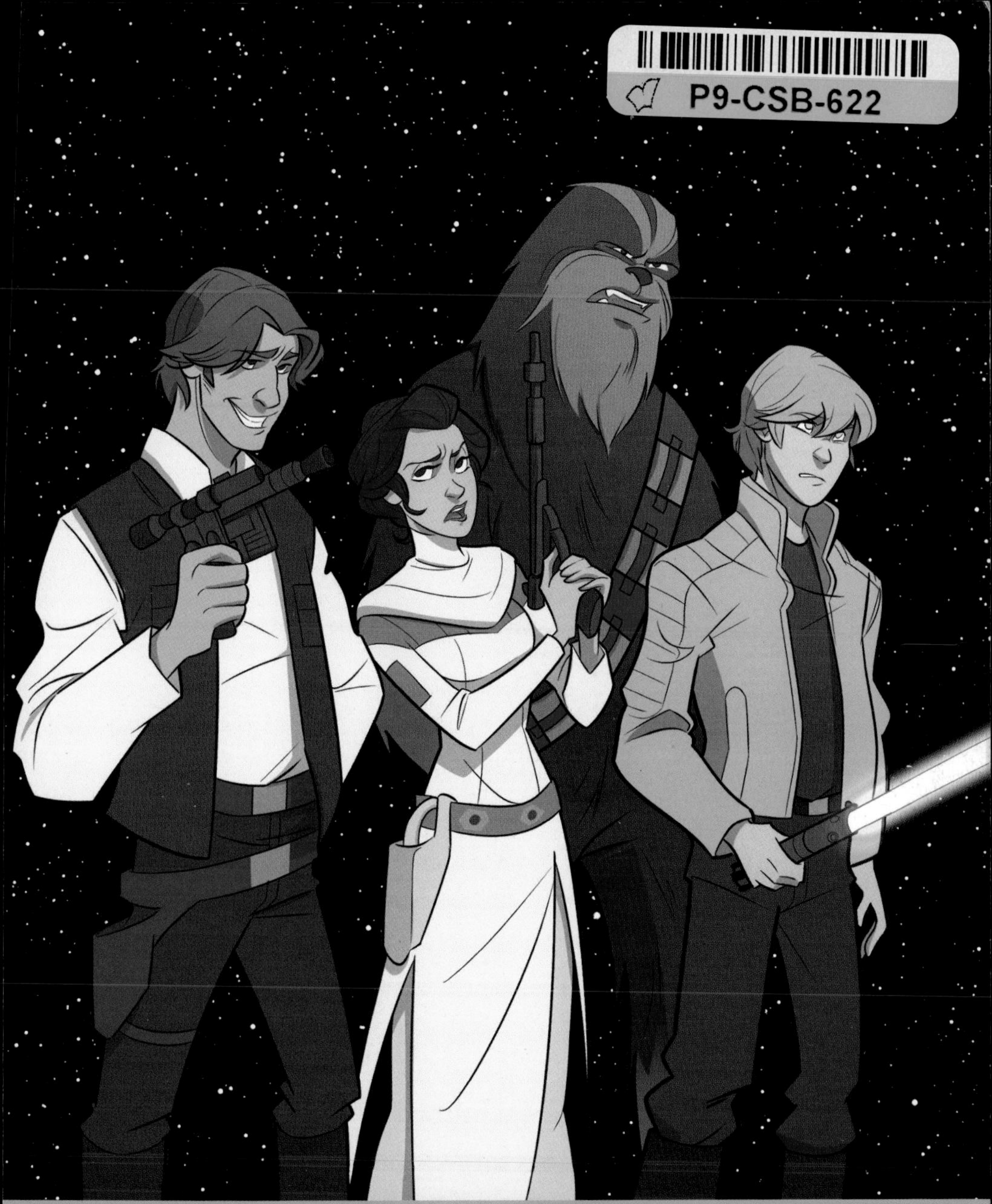

STAR WARS™ ADVENTURES

Flight of the Falcon

Facebook: **facebook.com/idwpublishing**
Twitter: **@idwpublishing**
YouTube: **youtube.com/idwpublishing**
Tumblr: **tumblr.idwpublishing.com**
Instagram: **instagram.com/idwpublishing**

ISBN: 978-1-68405-499-2   22 21 20 19   1 2 3 4

COVER ARTIST
PHILIP MURPHY

LETTERER
TOM B. LONG

SERIES ASSISTANT EDITOR
ELIZABETH BREI

SERIES EDITOR
DENTON J. TIPTON

COLLECTION EDITORS
JUSTIN EISINGER
& ALONZO SIMON

COLLECTION DESIGNER
CLYDE GRAPA

Originally published in STAR WARS ADVENTURES issues #14–18 and as STAR WARS ADVENTURES: FLIGHT OF THE FALCON.

Chris Ryall, President, Publisher, & CCO
John Barber, Editor-In-Chief
Robbie Robbins, EVP/Sr. Art Director
Cara Morrison, Chief Financial Officer
Matt Ruzicka, Chief Accounting Officer
David Hedgecock, Associate Publisher
Jerry Bennington, VP of New Product Development
Lorelei Bunjes, VP of Digital Services
Justin Eisinger, Editorial Director, Graphic Novels & Collections
Eric Moss, Senior Director, Licensing and Business Development

Ted Adams, IDW Founder

Lucasfilm Credits:
Senior Editor: Robert Simpson
Creative Director: Michael Siglain
Story Group: James Waugh, Leland Chee, Pablo Hidalgo, Matt Martin

Writer: Michael Moreci

Artist: Arianna Florean

Assistant Inker: Michele Pasta

Colorists: Arianna Florean, Adele Matera, and Mattia Iacono

Assistant Colorist: Sara Martinelli

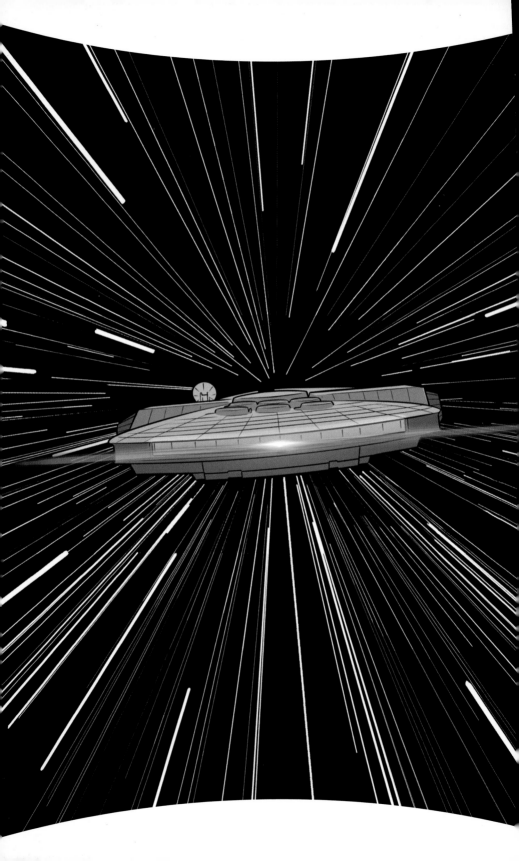

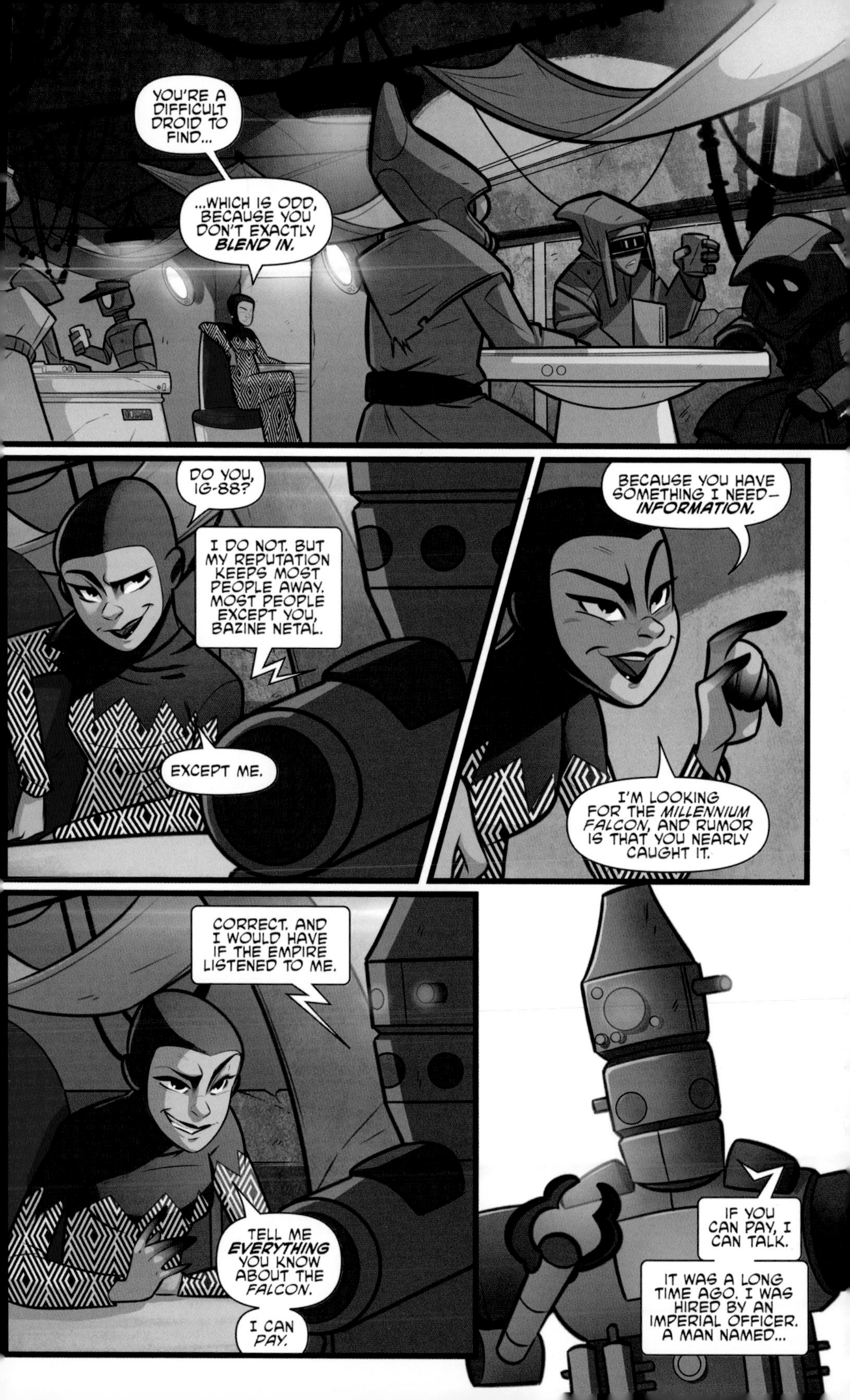

YOU'RE A DIFFICULT DROID TO FIND...
...WHICH IS ODD, BECAUSE YOU DON'T EXACTLY *BLEND IN.*
DO YOU, IG-88?
I DO NOT. BUT MY *REPUTATION* KEEPS MOST PEOPLE AWAY. MOST PEOPLE EXCEPT YOU, BAZINE NETAL.
EXCEPT ME.
BECAUSE YOU HAVE SOMETHING I NEED— *INFORMATION.*
I'M LOOKING FOR THE *MILLENNIUM FALCON*, AND RUMOR IS THAT YOU NEARLY CAUGHT IT.
CORRECT. AND I WOULD HAVE IF THE EMPIRE LISTENED TO ME.
TELL ME *EVERYTHING* YOU KNOW ABOUT THE *FALCON*.
I CAN *PAY.*
IF YOU CAN PAY, I CAN TALK.
IT WAS A LONG TIME AGO. I WAS HIRED BY AN IMPERIAL OFFICER. A MAN NAMED...

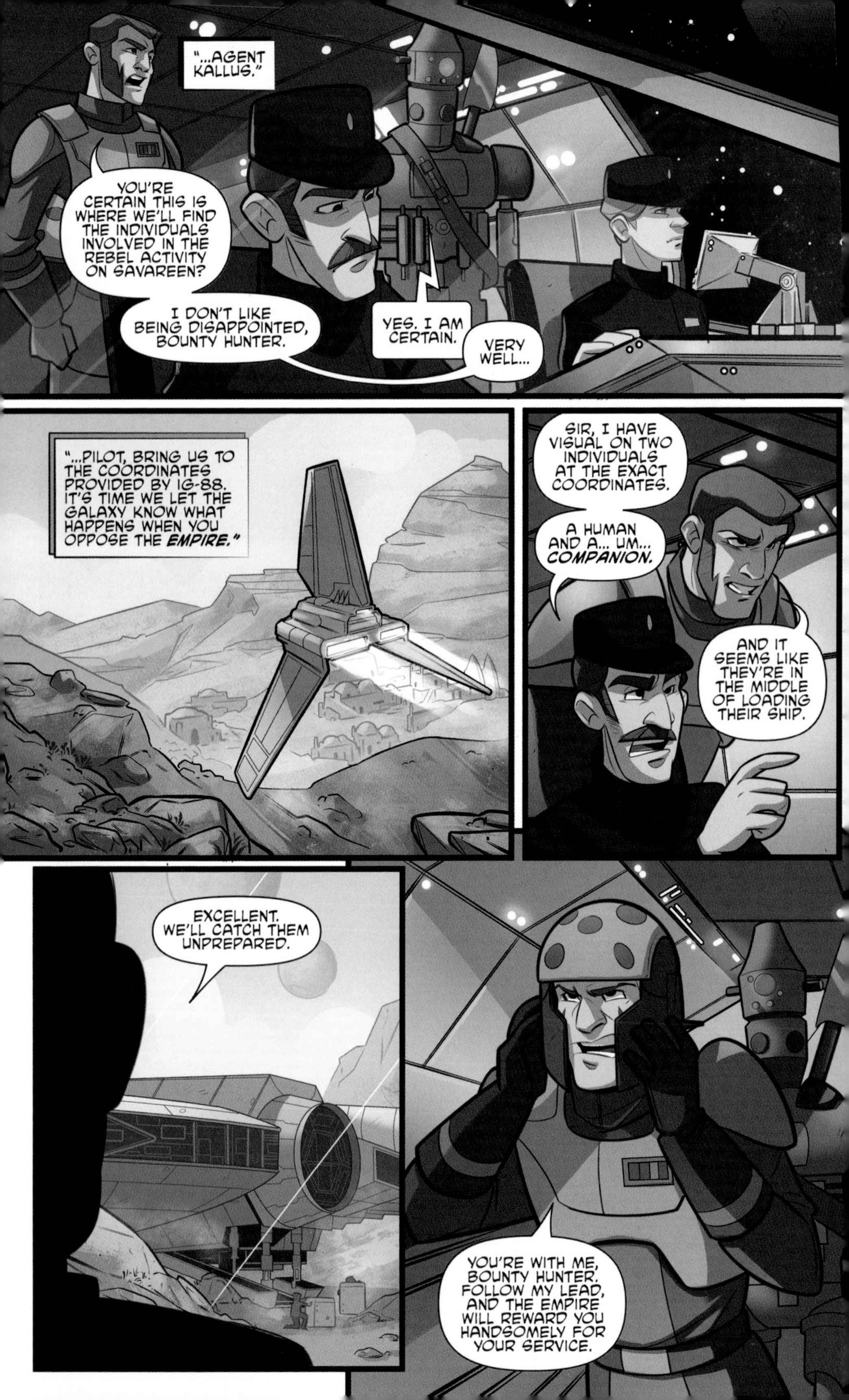
"...AGENT KALLUS."
YOU'RE CERTAIN THIS IS WHERE WE'LL FIND THE INDIVIDUALS INVOLVED IN THE REBEL ACTIVITY ON SAVAREEN?
I DON'T LIKE BEING DISAPPOINTED, BOUNTY HUNTER.
YES. I AM CERTAIN.
VERY WELL...
"...PILOT, BRING US TO THE COORDINATES PROVIDED BY IG-88. IT'S TIME WE LET THE GALAXY KNOW WHAT HAPPENS WHEN YOU OPPOSE THE EMPIRE."
SIR, I HAVE VISUAL ON TWO INDIVIDUALS AT THE EXACT COORDINATES.
A HUMAN AND A... UM... COMPANION.
AND IT SEEMS LIKE THEY'RE IN THE MIDDLE OF LOADING THEIR SHIP.
EXCELLENT. WE'LL CATCH THEM UNPREPARED.
YOU'RE WITH ME, BOUNTY HUNTER. FOLLOW MY LEAD, AND THE EMPIRE WILL REWARD YOU HANDSOMELY FOR YOUR SERVICE.

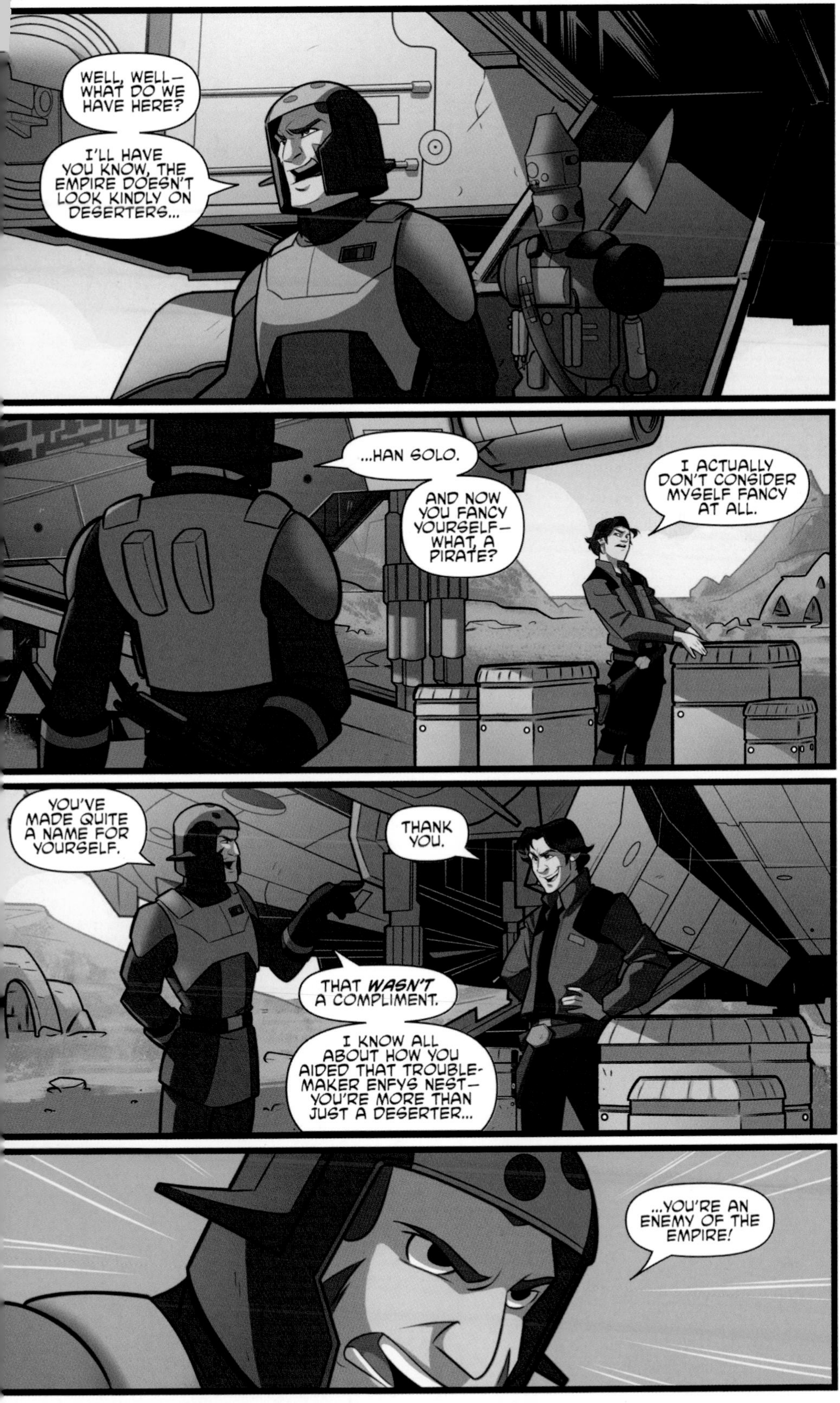
WELL, WELL— WHAT DO WE HAVE HERE?
I'LL HAVE YOU KNOW, THE EMPIRE DOESN'T LOOK KINDLY ON DESERTERS...
...HAN SOLO.
AND NOW YOU FANCY YOURSELF— WHAT, A PIRATE?
I ACTUALLY DON'T CONSIDER MYSELF FANCY AT ALL.
YOU'VE MADE QUITE A NAME FOR YOURSELF.
THANK YOU.
THAT *WASN'T* A COMPLIMENT.
I KNOW ALL ABOUT HOW YOU AIDED THAT TROUBLE-MAKER ENFYS NEST— YOU'RE MORE THAN JUST A DESERTER...
...YOU'RE AN ENEMY OF THE EMPIRE!

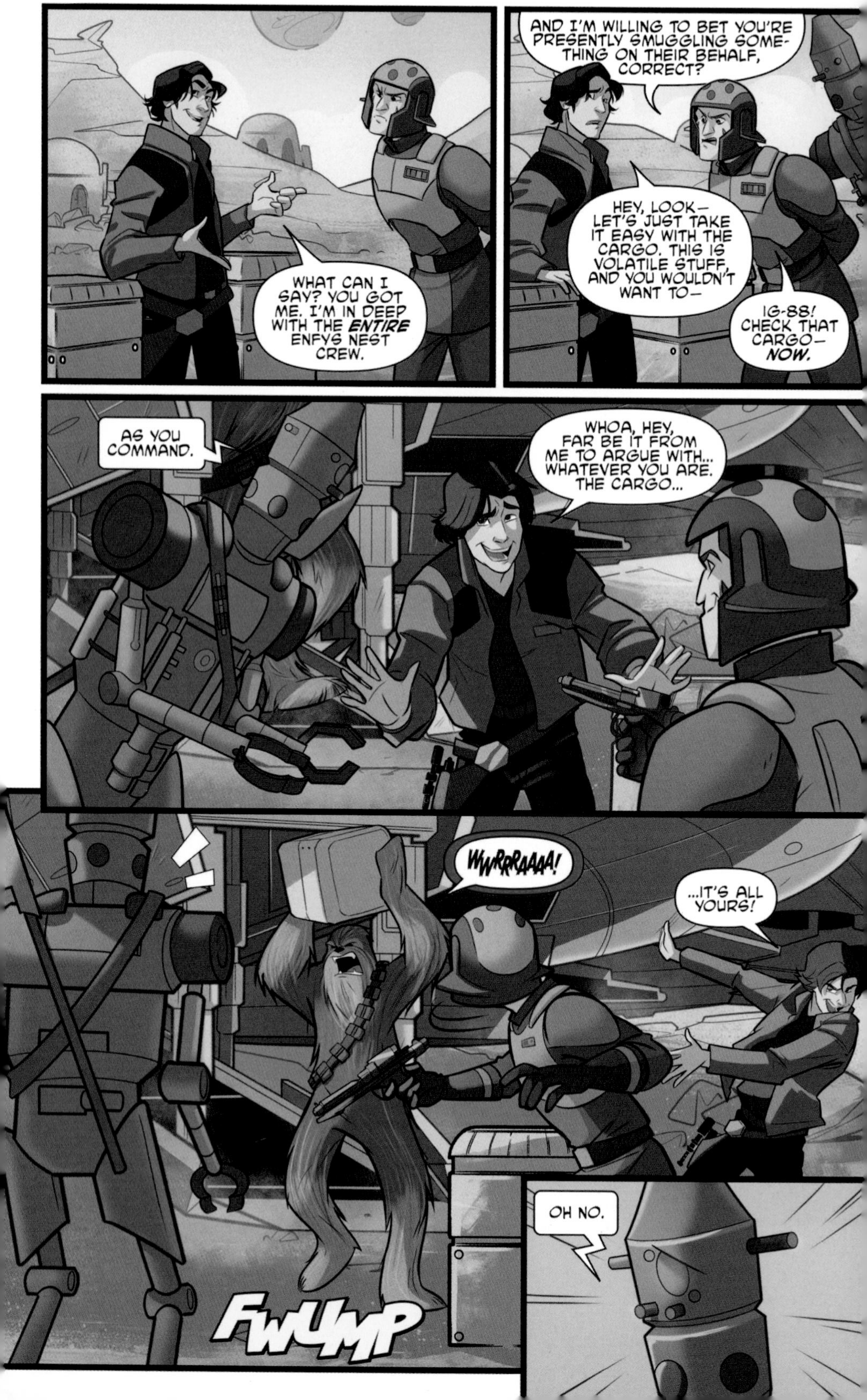

WHAT CAN I SAY? YOU GOT ME. I'M IN DEEP WITH THE *ENTIRE* ENFYS NEST CREW.
AND I'M WILLING TO BET YOU'RE PRESENTLY SMUGGLING SOMETHING ON THEIR BEHALF, CORRECT?
HEY, LOOK— LET'S JUST TAKE IT EASY WITH THE CARGO. THIS IS VOLATILE STUFF, AND YOU WOULDN'T WANT TO—
IG-88! CHECK THAT CARGO— *NOW.*
AS YOU COMMAND.
WHOA, HEY, FAR BE IT FROM ME TO ARGUE WITH... WHATEVER YOU ARE. THE CARGO...
WWRRRAAAA!
...IT'S ALL YOURS!
FWUMP
OH NO.

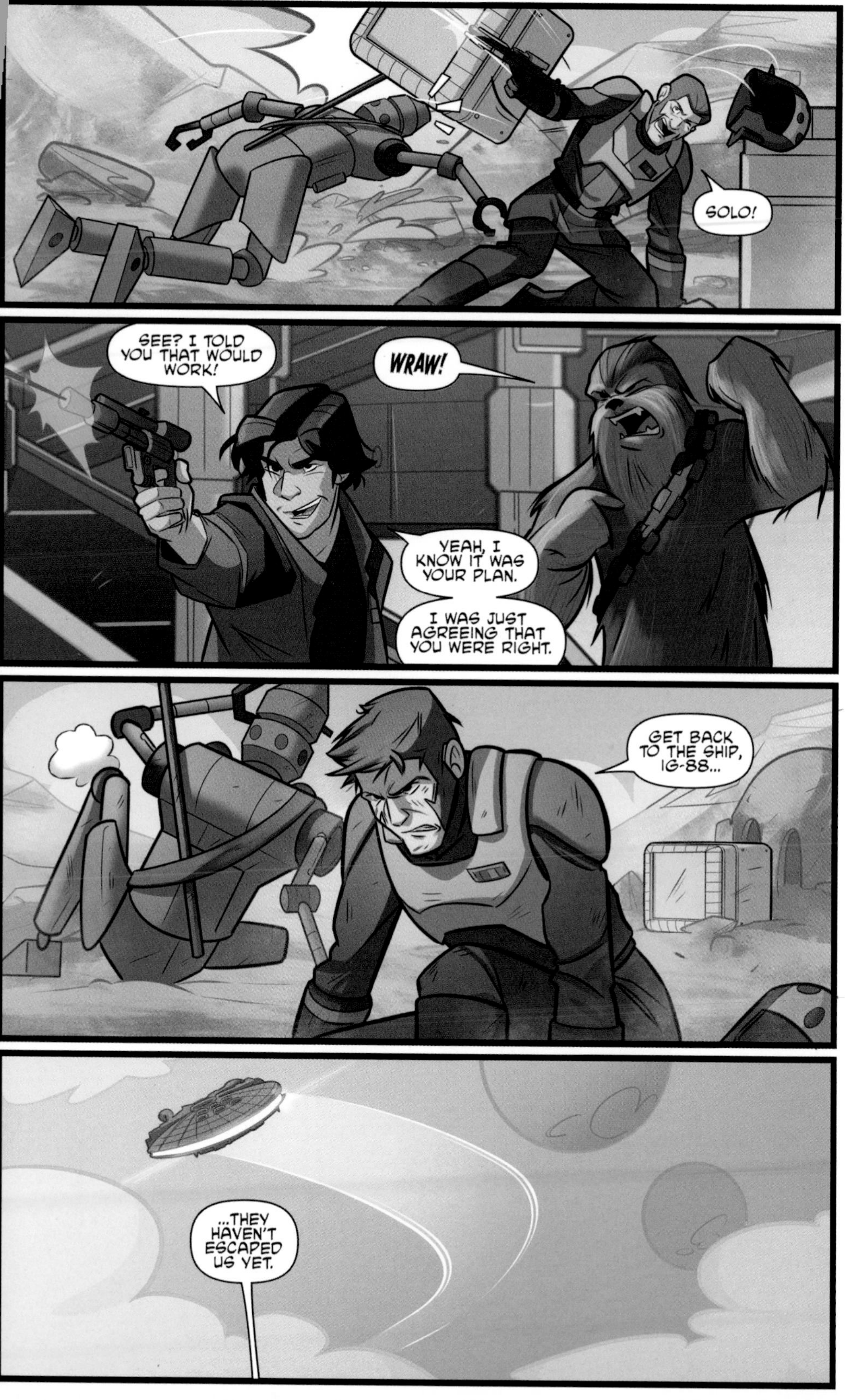
SOLO!
SEE? I TOLD YOU THAT WOULD WORK!
WRAW!
YEAH, I KNOW IT WAS YOUR PLAN.
I WAS JUST AGREEING THAT YOU WERE RIGHT.
GET BACK TO THE SHIP, IG-88...
...THEY HAVEN'T ESCAPED US YET.

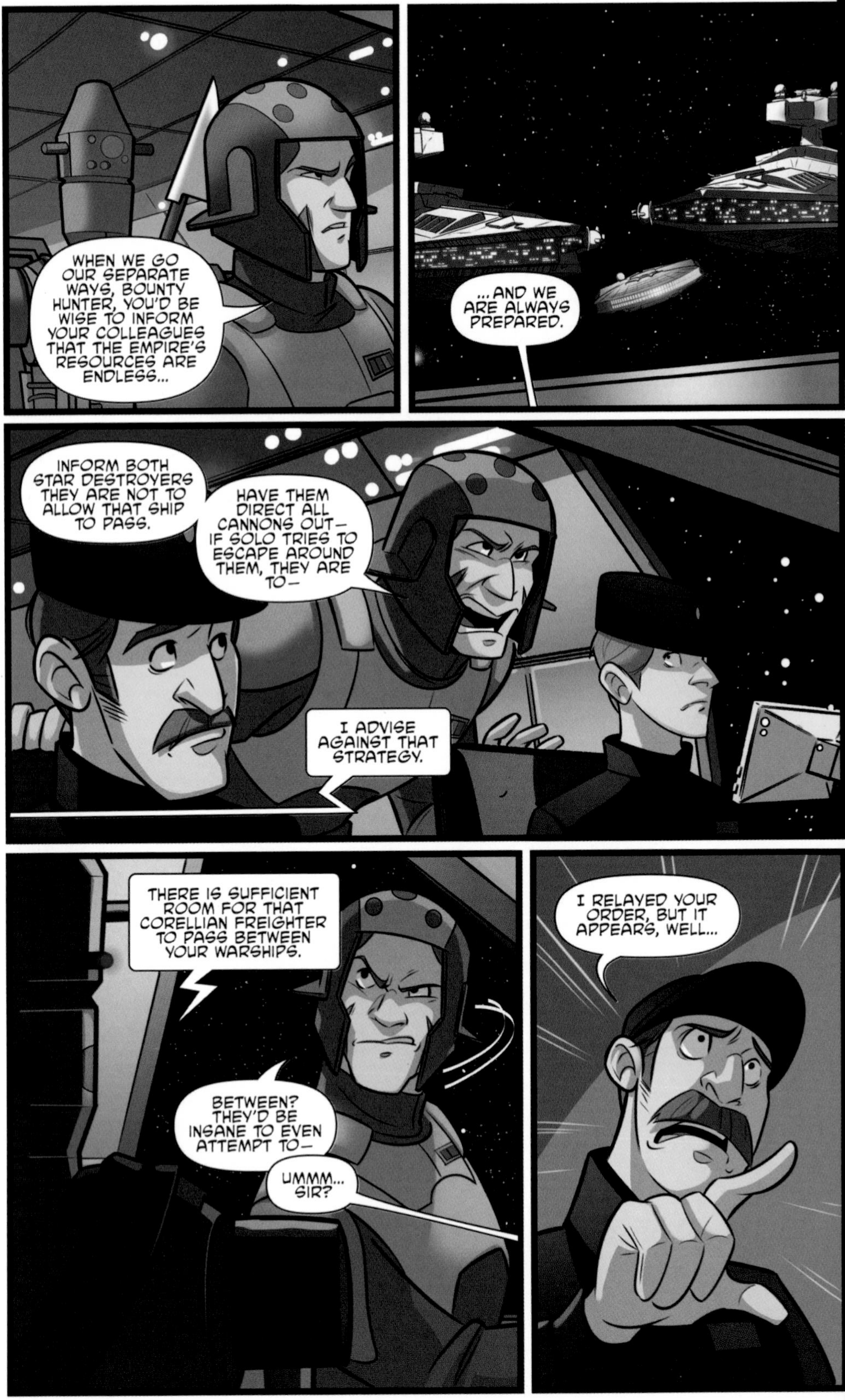
WHEN WE GO OUR SEPARATE WAYS, BOUNTY HUNTER, YOU'D BE WISE TO INFORM YOUR COLLEAGUES THAT THE EMPIRE'S RESOURCES ARE ENDLESS...
...AND WE ARE ALWAYS PREPARED.
INFORM BOTH STAR DESTROYERS THEY ARE NOT TO ALLOW THAT SHIP TO PASS.
HAVE THEM DIRECT ALL CANNONS OUT— IF SOLO TRIES TO ESCAPE AROUND THEM, THEY ARE TO—
I ADVISE AGAINST THAT STRATEGY.
THERE IS SUFFICIENT ROOM FOR THAT CORELLIAN FREIGHTER TO PASS BETWEEN YOUR WARSHIPS.
BETWEEN? THEY'D BE INSANE TO EVEN ATTEMPT TO—
UMMM... SIR?
I RELAYED YOUR ORDER, BUT IT APPEARS, WELL...

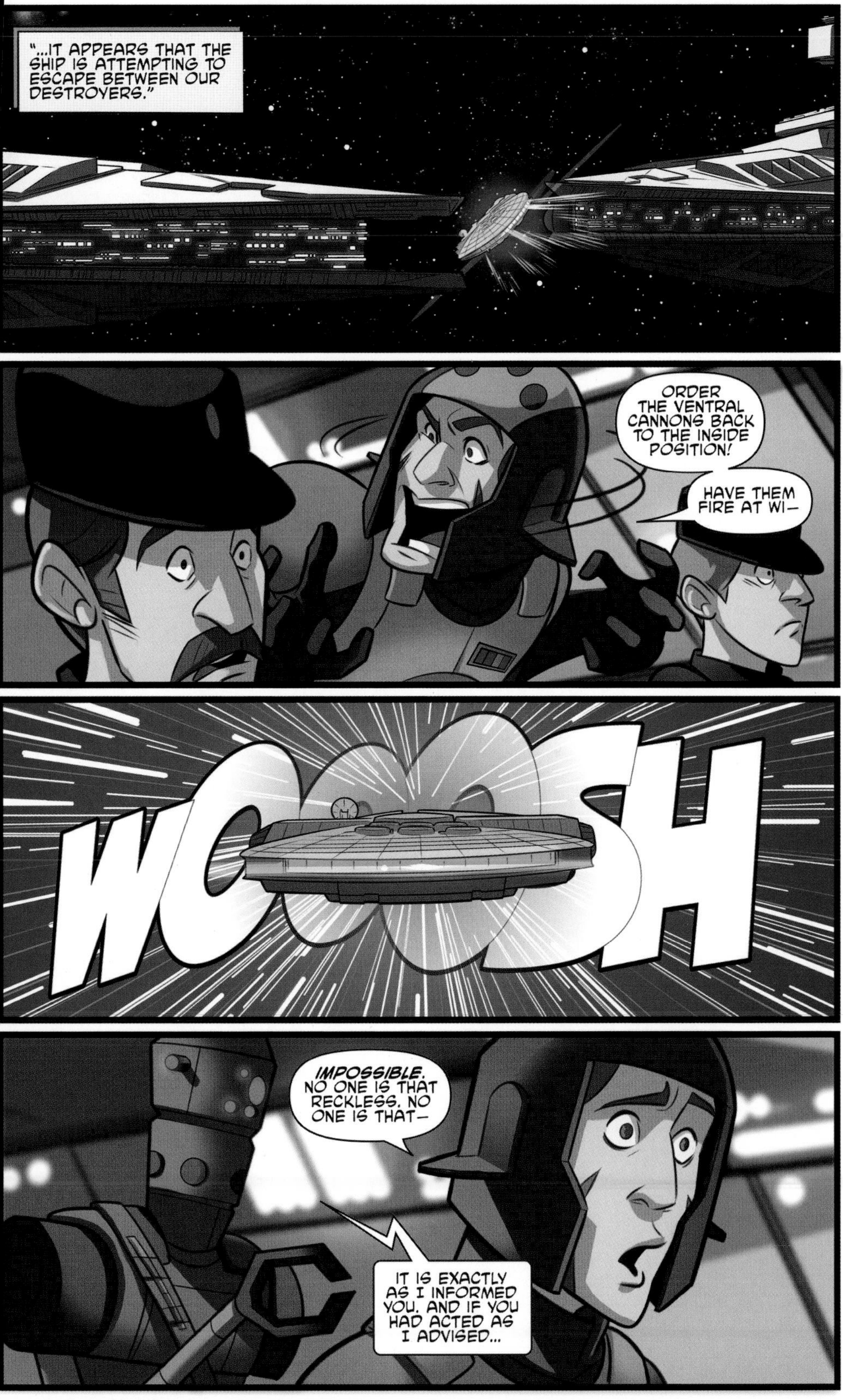
"...IT APPEARS THAT THE SHIP IS ATTEMPTING TO ESCAPE BETWEEN OUR DESTROYERS."
ORDER THE VENTRAL CANNONS BACK TO THE INSIDE POSITION!
HAVE THEM FIRE AT WI—
WOOOSH
IMPOSSIBLE. NO ONE IS THAT RECKLESS. NO ONE IS THAT—
IT IS EXACTLY AS I INFORMED YOU. AND IF YOU HAD ACTED AS I ADVISED...

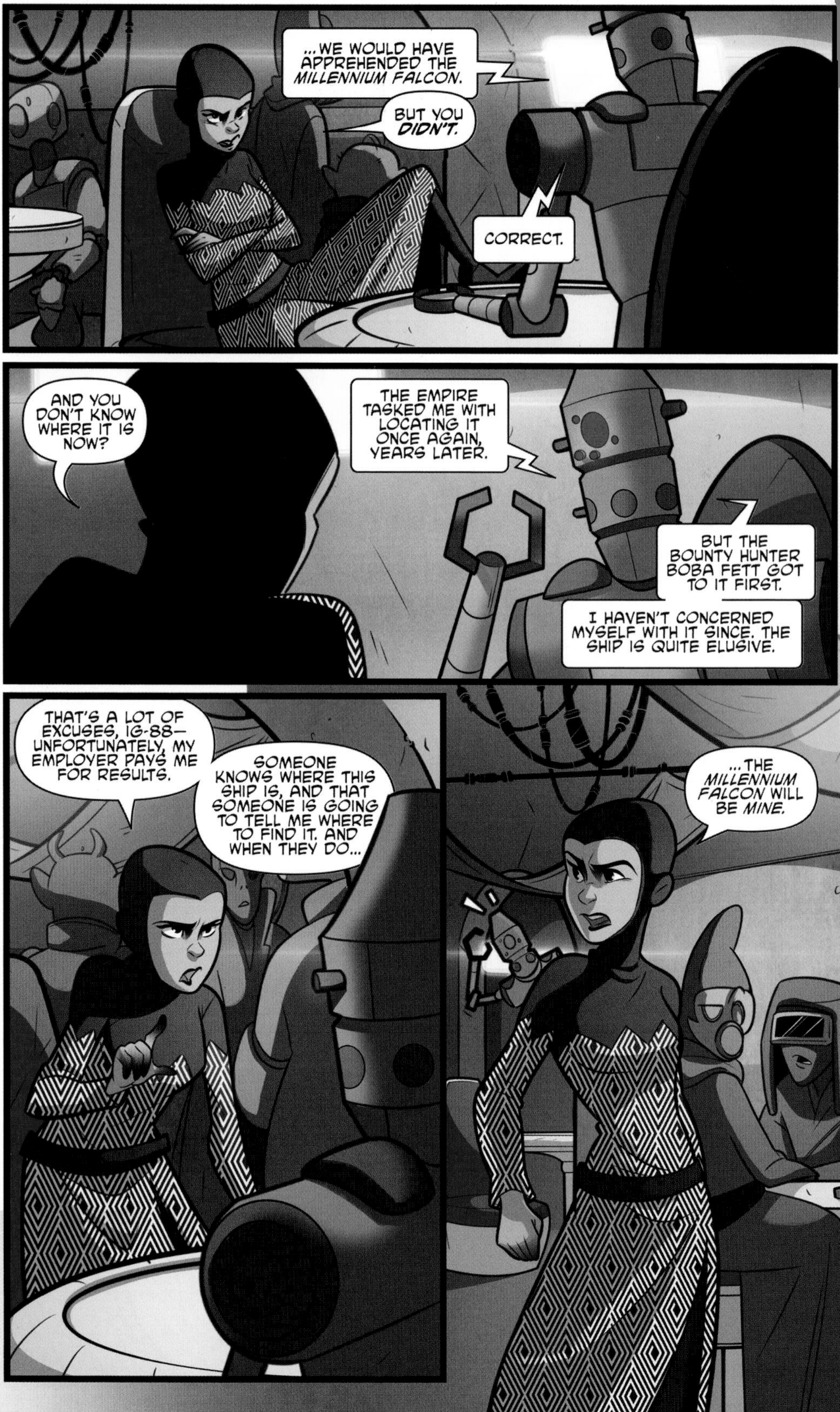
...WE WOULD HAVE APPREHENDED THE MILLENNIUM FALCON.
BUT YOU DIDN'T.
CORRECT.
AND YOU DON'T KNOW WHERE IT IS NOW?
THE EMPIRE TASKED ME WITH LOCATING IT ONCE AGAIN, YEARS LATER.
BUT THE BOUNTY HUNTER BOBA FETT GOT TO IT FIRST.
I HAVEN'T CONCERNED MYSELF WITH IT SINCE. THE SHIP IS QUITE ELUSIVE.
THAT'S A LOT OF EXCUSES, IG-88— UNFORTUNATELY, MY EMPLOYER PAYS ME FOR RESULTS.
SOMEONE KNOWS WHERE THIS SHIP IS, AND THAT SOMEONE IS GOING TO TELL ME WHERE TO FIND IT. AND WHEN THEY DO...
...THE MILLENNIUM FALCON WILL BE MINE.

"NO NO *NO*—DOC, ARE YOU *INTENTIONALLY* GETTING THE DETAILS WRONG?"

"I'M TELLING A STORY..."

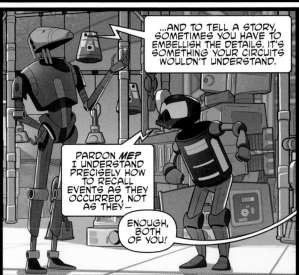

...AND TO TELL A STORY, SOMETIMES YOU HAVE TO EMBELLISH THE DETAILS. IT'S SOMETHING YOUR CIRCUITS WOULDN'T UNDERSTAND.

PARDON *ME?* I UNDERSTAND PRECISELY HOW TO RECALL EVENTS AS THEY OCCURRED, NOT AS THEY—

ENOUGH, BOTH OF YOU!

NEITHER OF YOU HAVE TOLD ME *ANYTHING.* SO EITHER GET TO THE STORY, AS IT *HAPPENED,* OR...

...WE'RE GOING TO HAVE A PROBLEM.

MAYBE IT'S BEST IF *YOU* TOLD THE STORY, TEETEE.

...VERY WELL.

YOU WISH TO KNOW OF OUR ENCOUNTER WITH THE *MILLENNIUM FALCON?*

UNLIKE MY COUNTERPART, I REMEMBER IT WITH ABSOLUTE CLARITY...

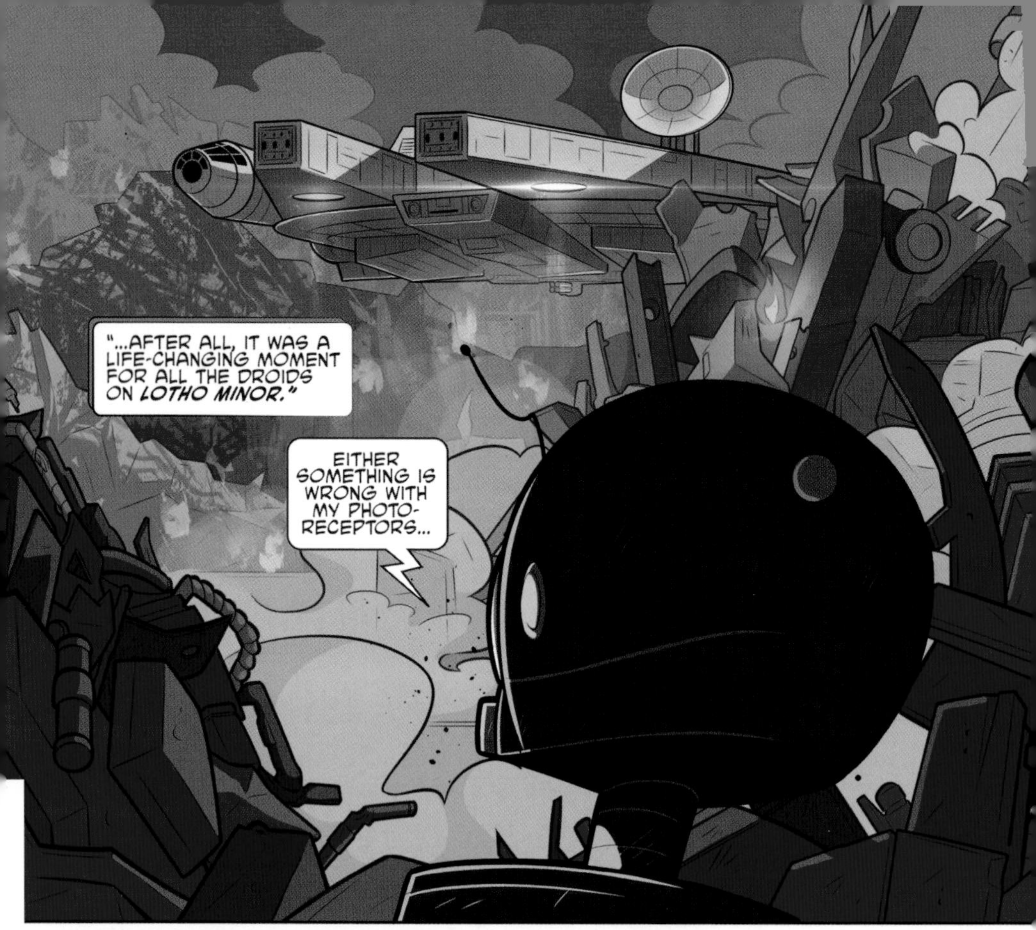
"...AFTER ALL, IT WAS A LIFE-CHANGING MOMENT FOR ALL THE DROIDS ON *LOTHO MINOR.*"
EITHER SOMETHING IS WRONG WITH MY PHOTO-RECEPTORS...

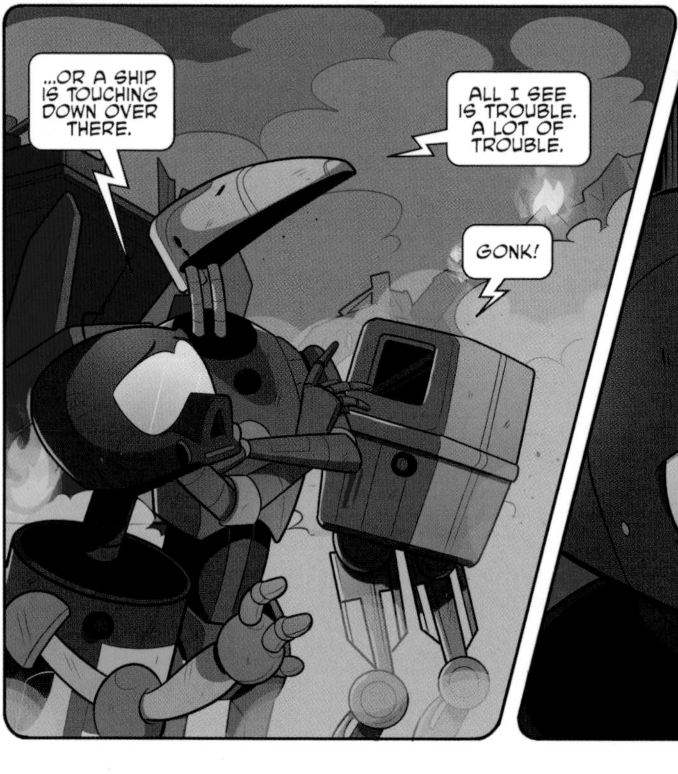
...OR A SHIP IS TOUCHING DOWN OVER THERE.
ALL I SEE IS TROUBLE. A LOT OF TROUBLE.
GONK!

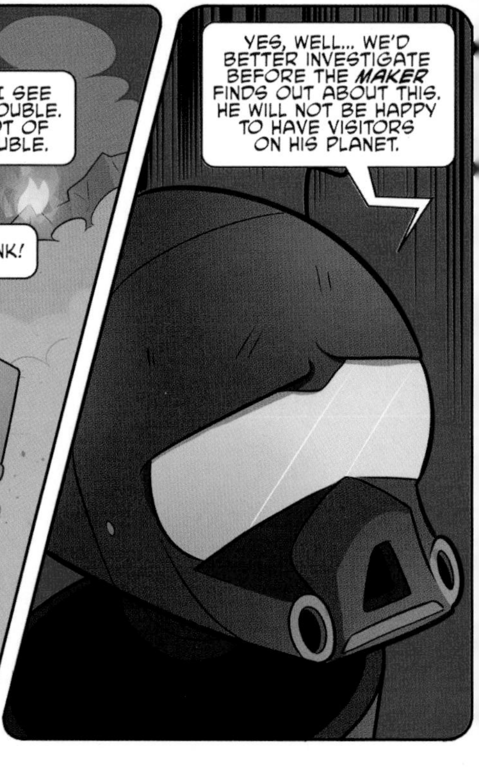
YES, WELL... WE'D BETTER INVESTIGATE BEFORE THE *MAKER* FINDS OUT ABOUT THIS. HE WILL NOT BE HAPPY TO HAVE VISITORS ON HIS PLANET.

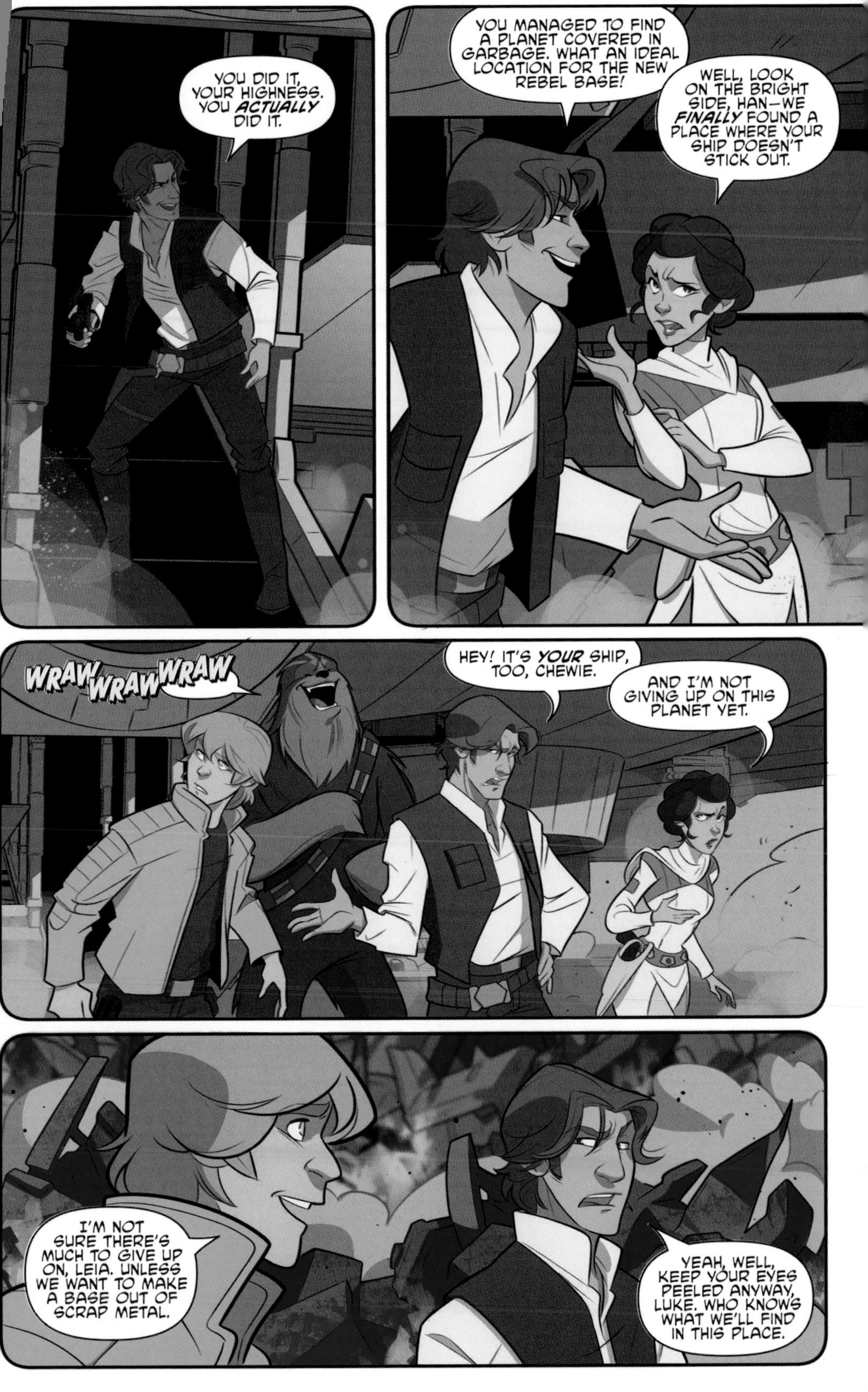
YOU DID IT, YOUR HIGHNESS. YOU ACTUALLY DID IT.
YOU MANAGED TO FIND A PLANET COVERED IN GARBAGE. WHAT AN IDEAL LOCATION FOR THE NEW REBEL BASE!
WELL, LOOK ON THE BRIGHT SIDE, HAN—WE FINALLY FOUND A PLACE WHERE YOUR SHIP DOESN'T STICK OUT.
WRAW WRAW WRAW
HEY! IT'S YOUR SHIP, TOO, CHEWIE.
AND I'M NOT GIVING UP ON THIS PLANET YET.
I'M NOT SURE THERE'S MUCH TO GIVE UP ON, LEIA. UNLESS WE WANT TO MAKE A BASE OUT OF SCRAP METAL.
YEAH, WELL, KEEP YOUR EYES PEELED ANYWAY, LUKE. WHO KNOWS WHAT WE'LL FIND IN THIS PLACE.

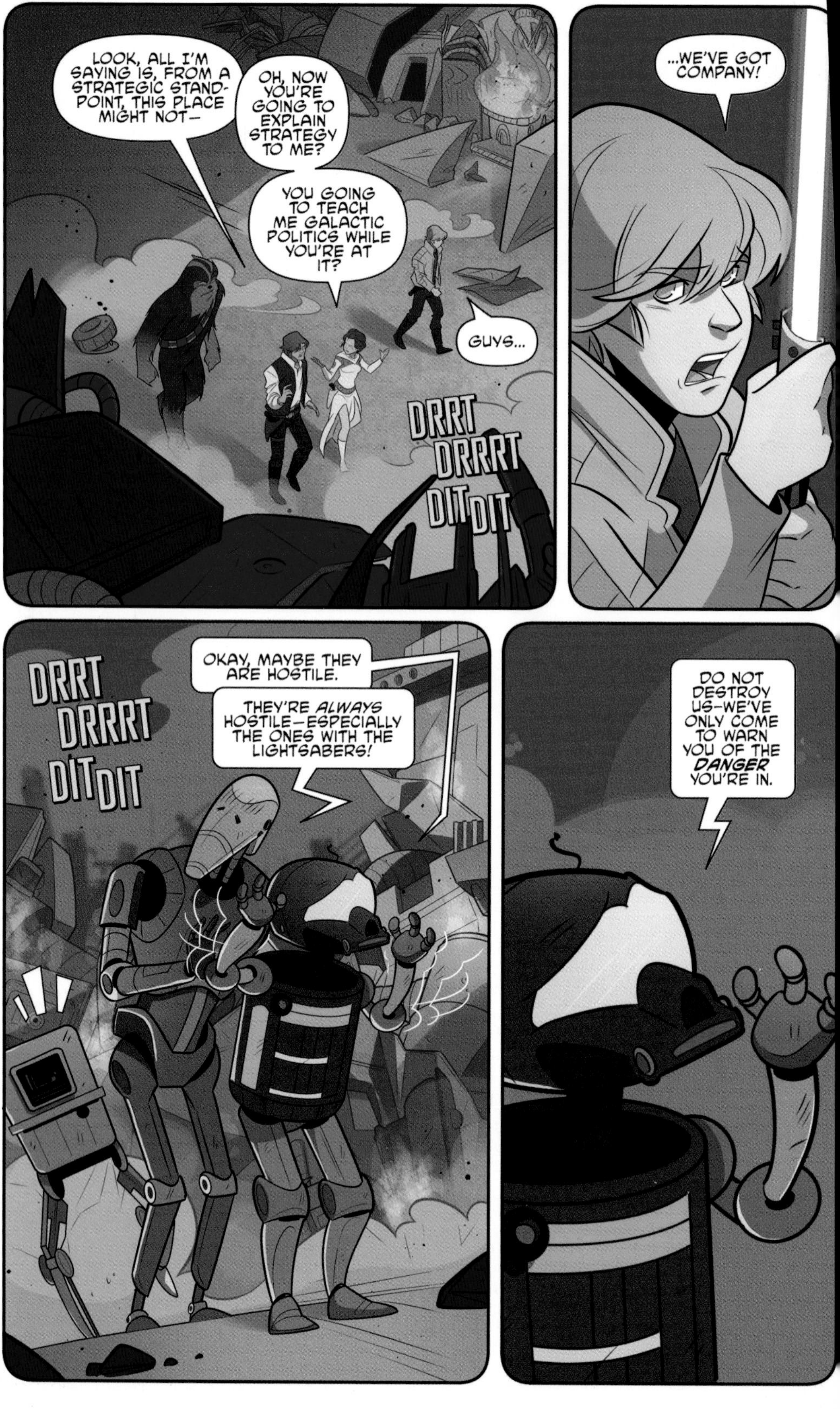
LOOK, ALL I'M SAYING IS, FROM A STRATEGIC STAND-POINT, THIS PLACE MIGHT NOT–
OH, NOW YOU'RE GOING TO EXPLAIN STRATEGY TO ME?
YOU GOING TO TEACH ME GALACTIC POLITICS WHILE YOU'RE AT IT?
GUYS...
DRRT DRRRT DITDIT
...WE'VE GOT COMPANY!
DRRT DRRRT DITDIT
OKAY, MAYBE THEY ARE HOSTILE.
THEY'RE *ALWAYS* HOSTILE–ESPECIALLY THE ONES WITH THE LIGHTSABERS!
DO NOT DESTROY US–WE'VE ONLY COME TO WARN YOU OF THE ***DANGER*** YOU'RE IN.

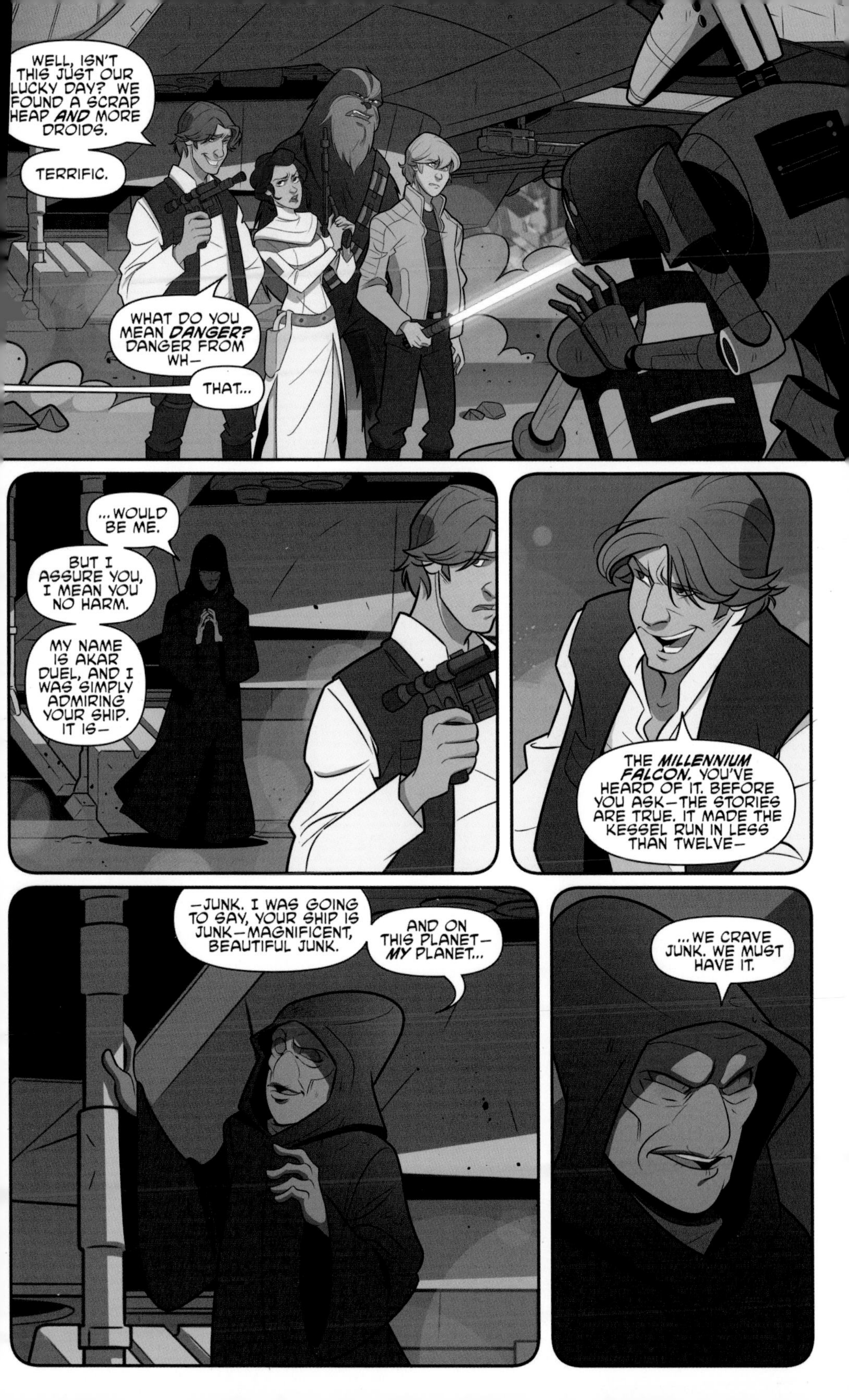
WELL, ISN'T THIS JUST OUR LUCKY DAY? WE FOUND A SCRAP HEAP *AND* MORE DROIDS.
TERRIFIC.
WHAT DO YOU MEAN *DANGER?* DANGER FROM WH—
THAT...
...WOULD BE ME.
BUT I ASSURE YOU, I MEAN YOU NO HARM.
MY NAME IS AKAR DUEL, AND I WAS SIMPLY ADMIRING YOUR SHIP. IT IS—
THE *MILLENNIUM FALCON.* YOU'VE HEARD OF IT. BEFORE YOU ASK—THE STORIES ARE TRUE. IT MADE THE KESSEL RUN IN LESS THAN TWELVE—
—JUNK. I WAS GOING TO SAY, YOUR SHIP IS JUNK—MAGNIFICENT, BEAUTIFUL JUNK.
AND ON THIS PLANET—*MY* PLANET...
...WE CRAVE JUNK. WE MUST HAVE IT.

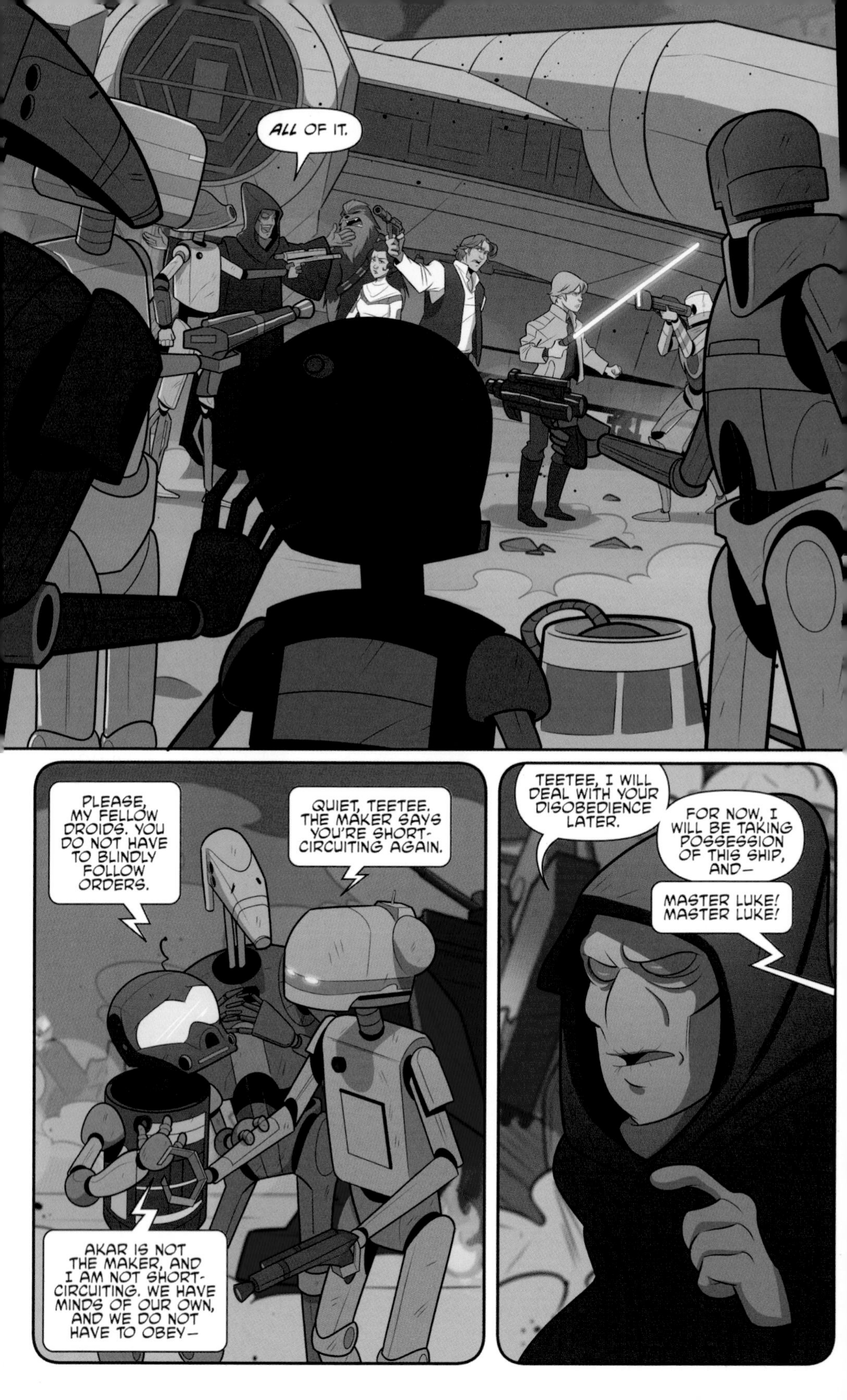
ALL OF IT.
PLEASE, MY FELLOW DROIDS. YOU DO NOT HAVE TO BLINDLY FOLLOW ORDERS.
QUIET, TEETEE. THE MAKER SAYS YOU'RE SHORT-CIRCUITING AGAIN.
AKAR IS NOT THE MAKER, AND I AM NOT SHORT-CIRCUITING. WE HAVE MINDS OF OUR OWN, AND WE DO NOT HAVE TO OBEY—
TEETEE, I WILL DEAL WITH YOUR DISOBEDIENCE LATER.
FOR NOW, I WILL BE TAKING POSSESSION OF THIS SHIP, AND—
MASTER LUKE! MASTER LUKE!

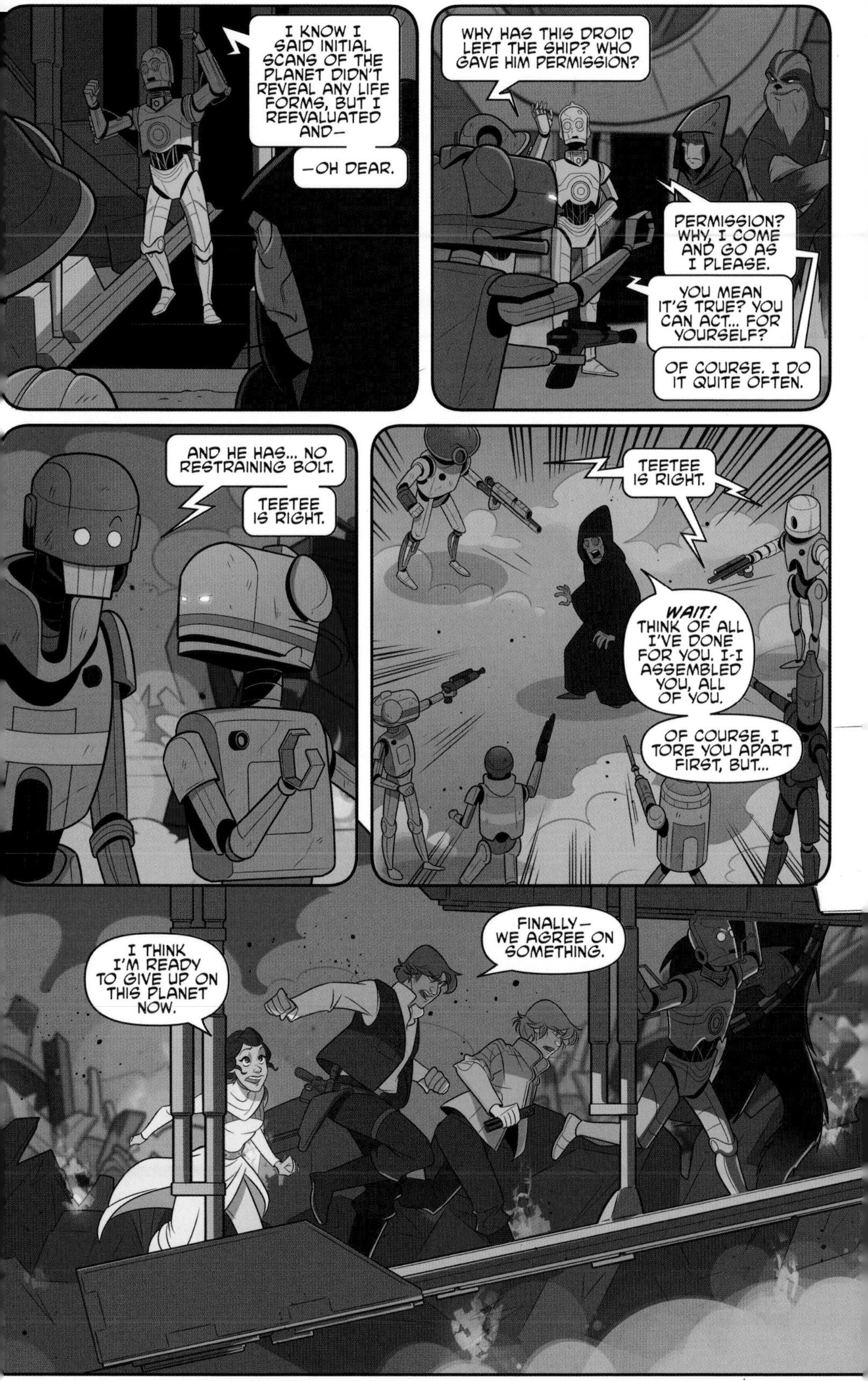
I KNOW I SAID INITIAL SCANS OF THE PLANET DIDN'T REVEAL ANY LIFE FORMS, BUT I REEVALUATED AND—
—OH DEAR.
WHY HAS THIS DROID LEFT THE SHIP? WHO GAVE HIM PERMISSION?
PERMISSION? WHY, I COME AND GO AS I PLEASE.
YOU MEAN IT'S TRUE? YOU CAN ACT... FOR YOURSELF?
OF COURSE. I DO IT QUITE OFTEN.
AND HE HAS... NO RESTRAINING BOLT.
TEETEE IS RIGHT.
TEETEE IS RIGHT.
WAIT! THINK OF ALL I'VE DONE FOR YOU. I-I ASSEMBLED YOU, ALL OF YOU.
OF COURSE, I TORE YOU APART FIRST, BUT...
I THINK I'M READY TO GIVE UP ON THIS PLANET NOW.
FINALLY— WE AGREE ON SOMETHING.

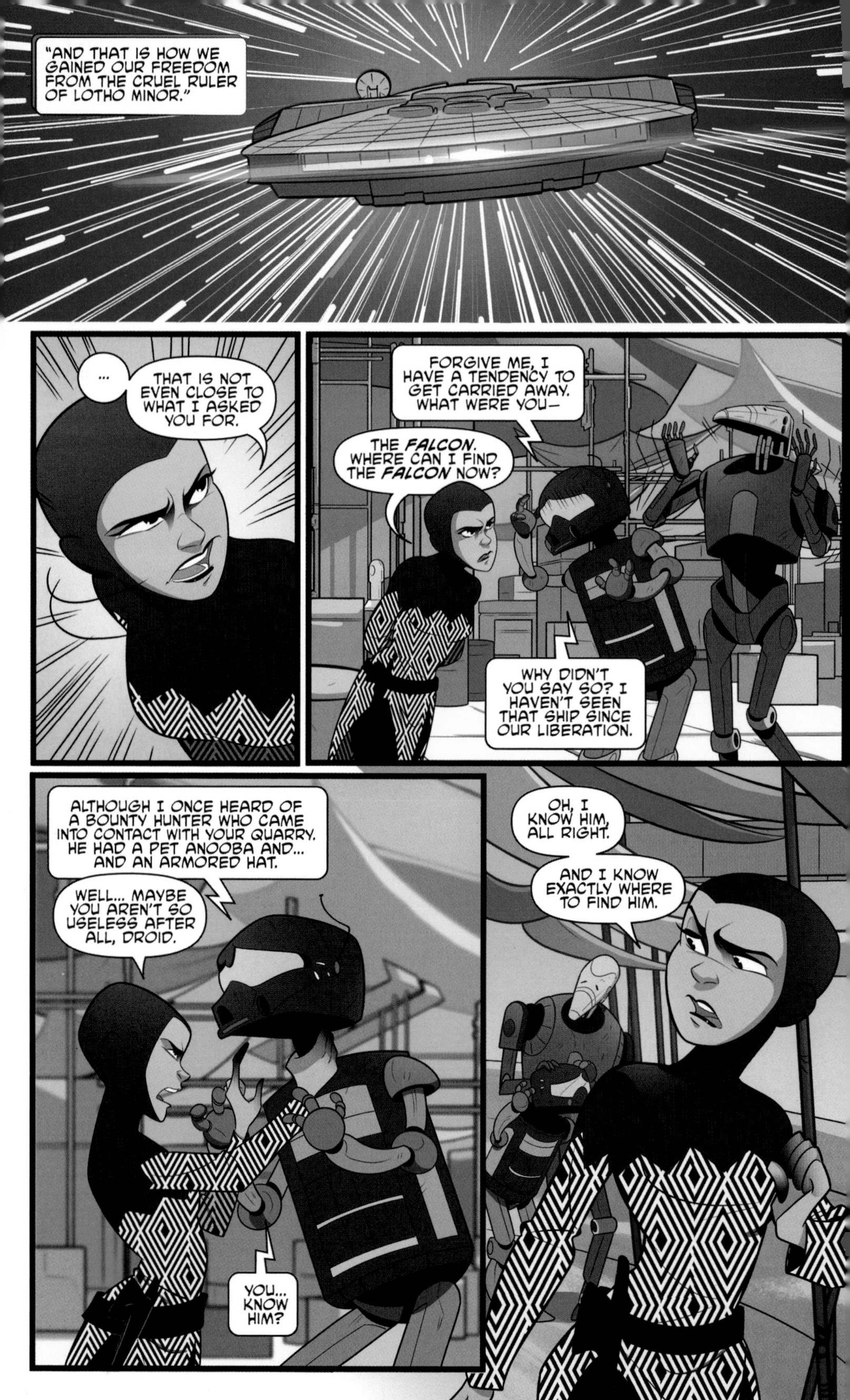
"AND THAT IS HOW WE GAINED OUR FREEDOM FROM THE CRUEL RULER OF LOTHO MINOR."
...
THAT IS NOT EVEN CLOSE TO WHAT I ASKED YOU FOR.
FORGIVE ME, I HAVE A TENDENCY TO GET CARRIED AWAY. WHAT WERE YOU—
THE FALCON. WHERE CAN I FIND THE FALCON NOW?
WHY DIDN'T YOU SAY SO? I HAVEN'T SEEN THAT SHIP SINCE OUR LIBERATION.
ALTHOUGH I ONCE HEARD OF A BOUNTY HUNTER WHO CAME INTO CONTACT WITH YOUR QUARRY. HE HAD A PET ANOOBA AND... AND AN ARMORED HAT.
WELL... MAYBE YOU AREN'T SO USELESS AFTER ALL, DROID.
YOU... KNOW HIM?
OH, I KNOW HIM, ALL RIGHT.
AND I KNOW EXACTLY WHERE TO FIND HIM.

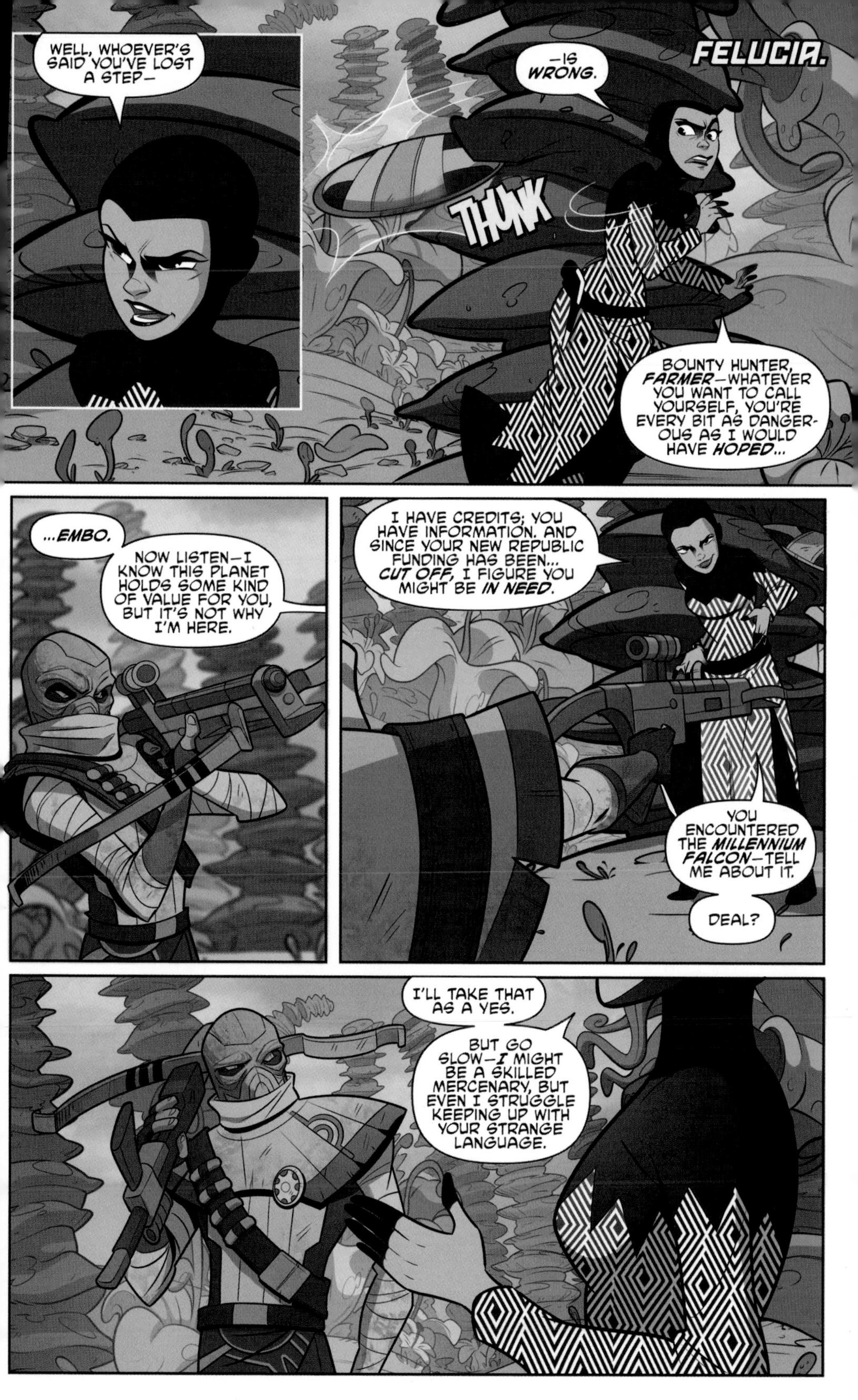

WELL, WHOEVER'S SAID YOU'VE LOST A STEP—
—IS *WRONG*.
FELUCIA.
THUNK
BOUNTY HUNTER, *FARMER*—WHATEVER YOU WANT TO CALL YOURSELF, YOU'RE EVERY BIT AS DANGER-OUS AS I WOULD HAVE *HOPED*...
...*EMBO.*
NOW LISTEN—I KNOW THIS PLANET HOLDS SOME KIND OF VALUE FOR YOU, BUT IT'S NOT WHY I'M HERE.
I HAVE CREDITS; YOU HAVE INFORMATION. AND SINCE YOUR NEW REPUBLIC FUNDING HAS BEEN... *CUT OFF*, I FIGURE YOU MIGHT BE *IN NEED*.
YOU ENCOUNTERED THE *MILLENNIUM FALCON*—TELL ME ABOUT IT.
DEAL?
I'LL TAKE THAT AS A YES.
BUT GO SLOW—*I* MIGHT BE A SKILLED MERCENARY, BUT EVEN I STRUGGLE KEEPING UP WITH YOUR STRANGE LANGUAGE.

"TERRIFIC. JUST *TERRIFIC.*

"WE MAKE A SIMPLE FUEL STOP AND THIS IS WHAT WE GET."

ᕮᐁᐊᑫ ᕮᐁᑫᕮᕬ ᕮᐊᐅᐊᒍᐊᑎᐅᕬᕮ

WHAT'S *WRONG* WITH IT? IT'D BE EASIER TO SAY WHAT'S RIGHT WITH IT.

THE WAY *HAN'S* MAINTAINED THIS SHIP, WE'RE LUCKY WE DIDN'T STALL OUT WHILE INSIDE THE *DEATH STAR.*

LOOK, WHY DON'T YOU GO BACK TO THE MARKET, PICK UP SOME SUPPLIES. I'LL WORK ON GETTING US OUT OF HERE.

ᐁ ᐊᐅᕮᕮᕮ

YEAH— YOU CAN SAY THAT *AGAIN.*

WHAT DID THAT NO-GOOD PIRATE DO TO YOU?

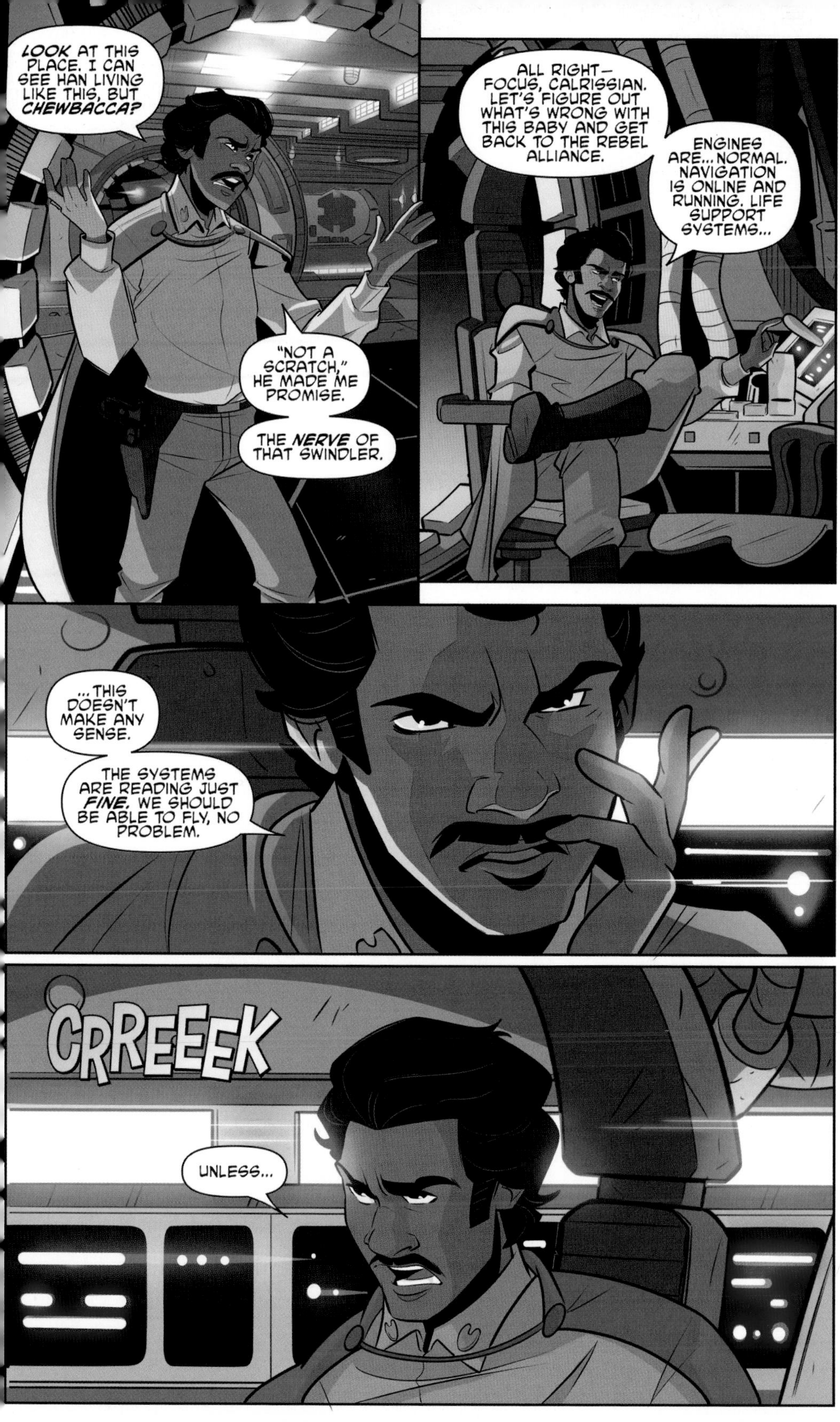
LOOK AT THIS PLACE. I CAN SEE HAN LIVING LIKE THIS, BUT CHEWBACCA?
"NOT A SCRATCH," HE MADE ME PROMISE.
THE NERVE OF THAT SWINDLER.
ALL RIGHT— FOCUS, CALRISSIAN. LET'S FIGURE OUT WHAT'S WRONG WITH THIS BABY AND GET BACK TO THE REBEL ALLIANCE.
ENGINES ARE... NORMAL. NAVIGATION IS ONLINE AND RUNNING. LIFE SUPPORT SYSTEMS...
...THIS DOESN'T MAKE ANY SENSE.
THE SYSTEMS ARE READING JUST FINE. WE SHOULD BE ABLE TO FLY, NO PROBLEM.
CRREEEK
UNLESS...

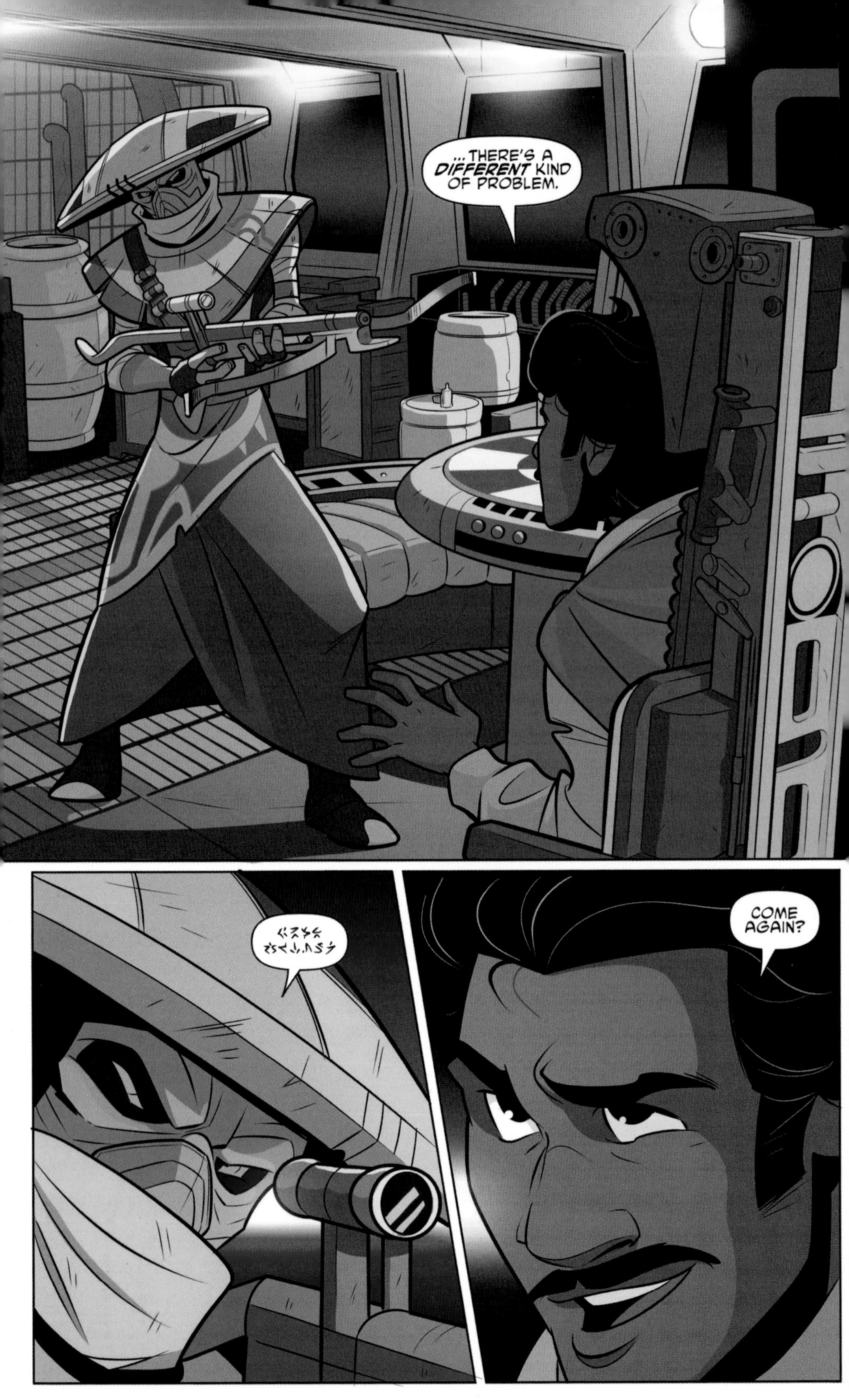
...THERE'S A *DIFFERENT* KIND OF PROBLEM.
COME AGAIN?

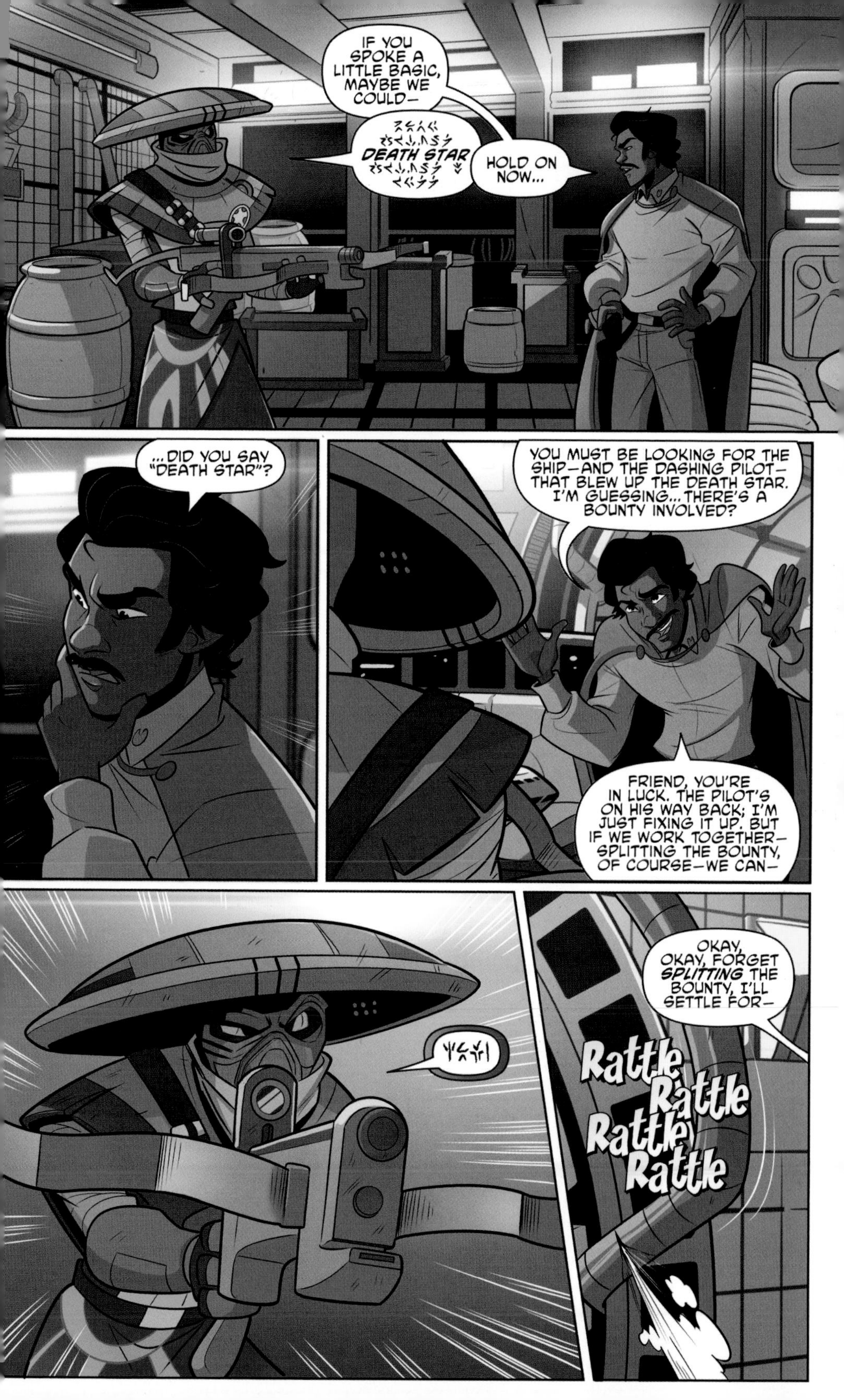
IF YOU SPOKE A LITTLE BASIC, MAYBE WE COULD—
DEATH STAR
HOLD ON NOW...
...DID YOU SAY "DEATH STAR"?
YOU MUST BE LOOKING FOR THE SHIP—AND THE DASHING PILOT—THAT BLEW UP THE DEATH STAR. I'M GUESSING... THERE'S A BOUNTY INVOLVED?
FRIEND, YOU'RE IN LUCK. THE PILOT'S ON HIS WAY BACK; I'M JUST FIXING IT UP. BUT IF WE WORK TOGETHER—SPLITTING THE BOUNTY, OF COURSE—WE CAN—
OKAY, OKAY, FORGET *SPLITTING* THE BOUNTY, I'LL SETTLE FOR—
Rattle Rattle Rattle Rattle

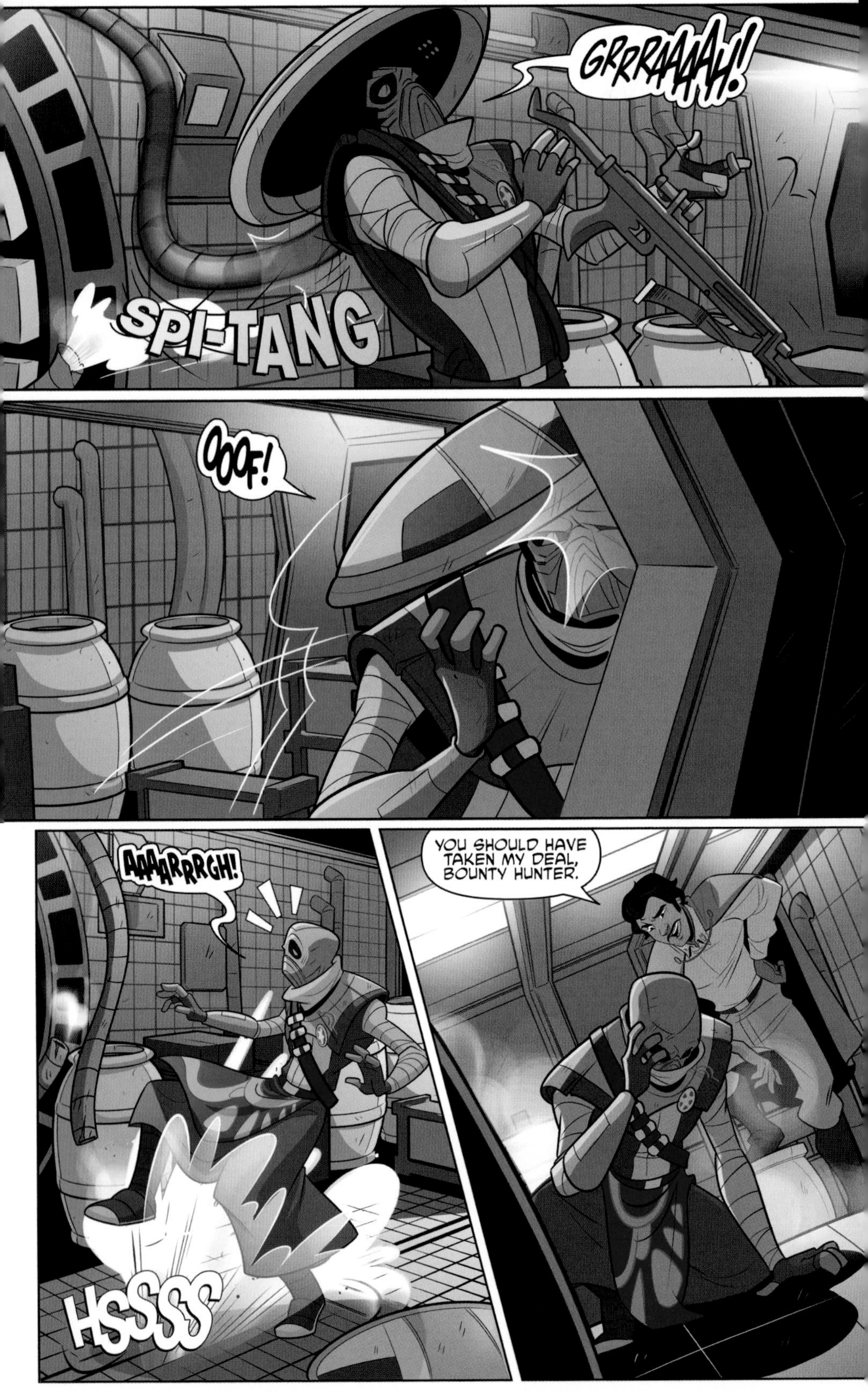
GRRRAAAAAH!
SPI-TANG
OOOF!
AAAARRRGH!
HSSSS
YOU SHOULD HAVE TAKEN MY DEAL, BOUNTY HUNTER.

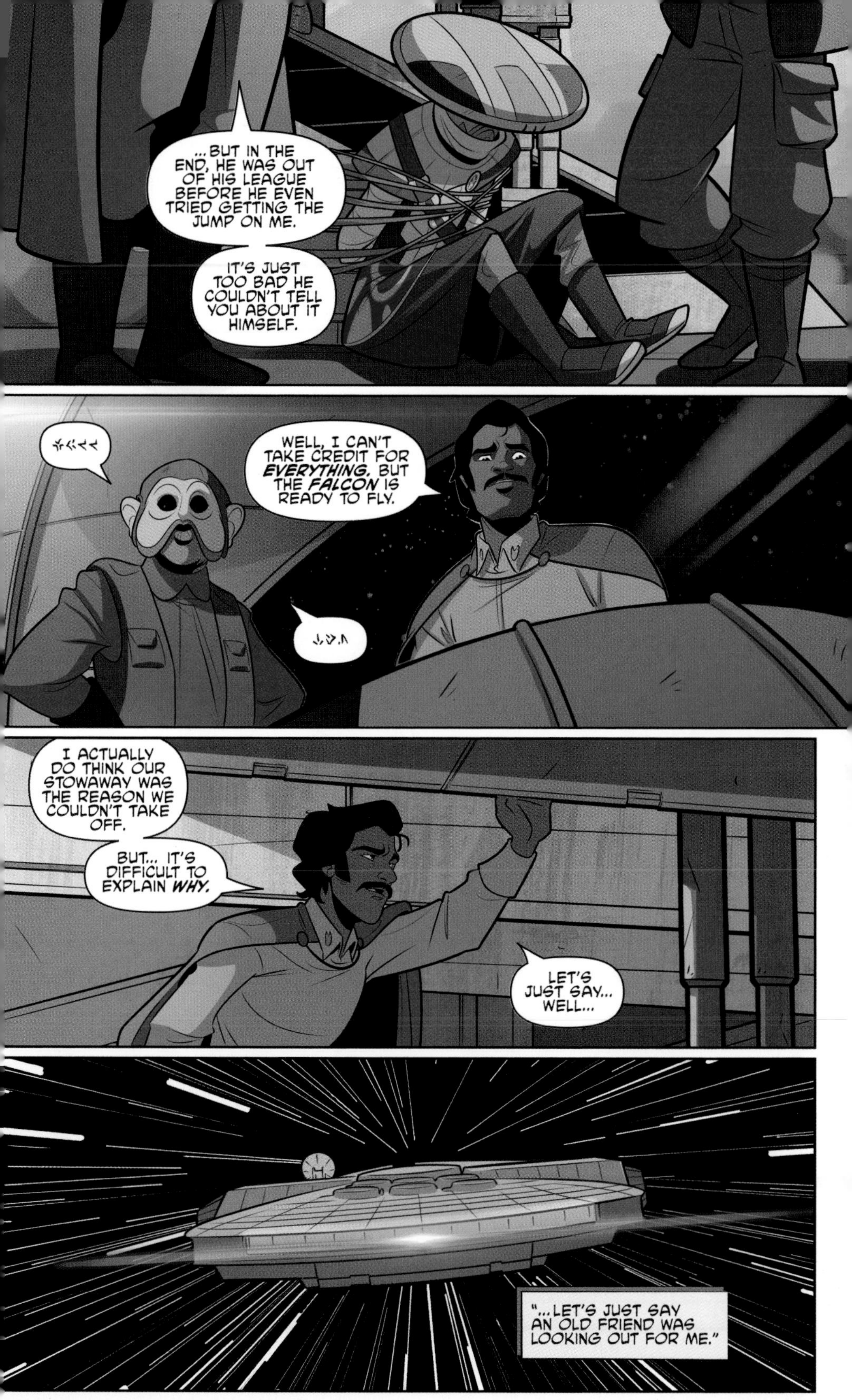
...BUT IN THE END, HE WAS OUT OF HIS LEAGUE BEFORE HE EVEN TRIED GETTING THE JUMP ON ME.
IT'S JUST TOO BAD HE COULDN'T TELL YOU ABOUT IT HIMSELF.
WELL, I CAN'T TAKE CREDIT FOR EVERYTHING, BUT THE FALCON IS READY TO FLY.
I ACTUALLY DO THINK OUR STOWAWAY WAS THE REASON WE COULDN'T TAKE OFF.
BUT... IT'S DIFFICULT TO EXPLAIN WHY.
LET'S JUST SAY... WELL...
"...LET'S JUST SAY AN OLD FRIEND WAS LOOKING OUT FOR ME."

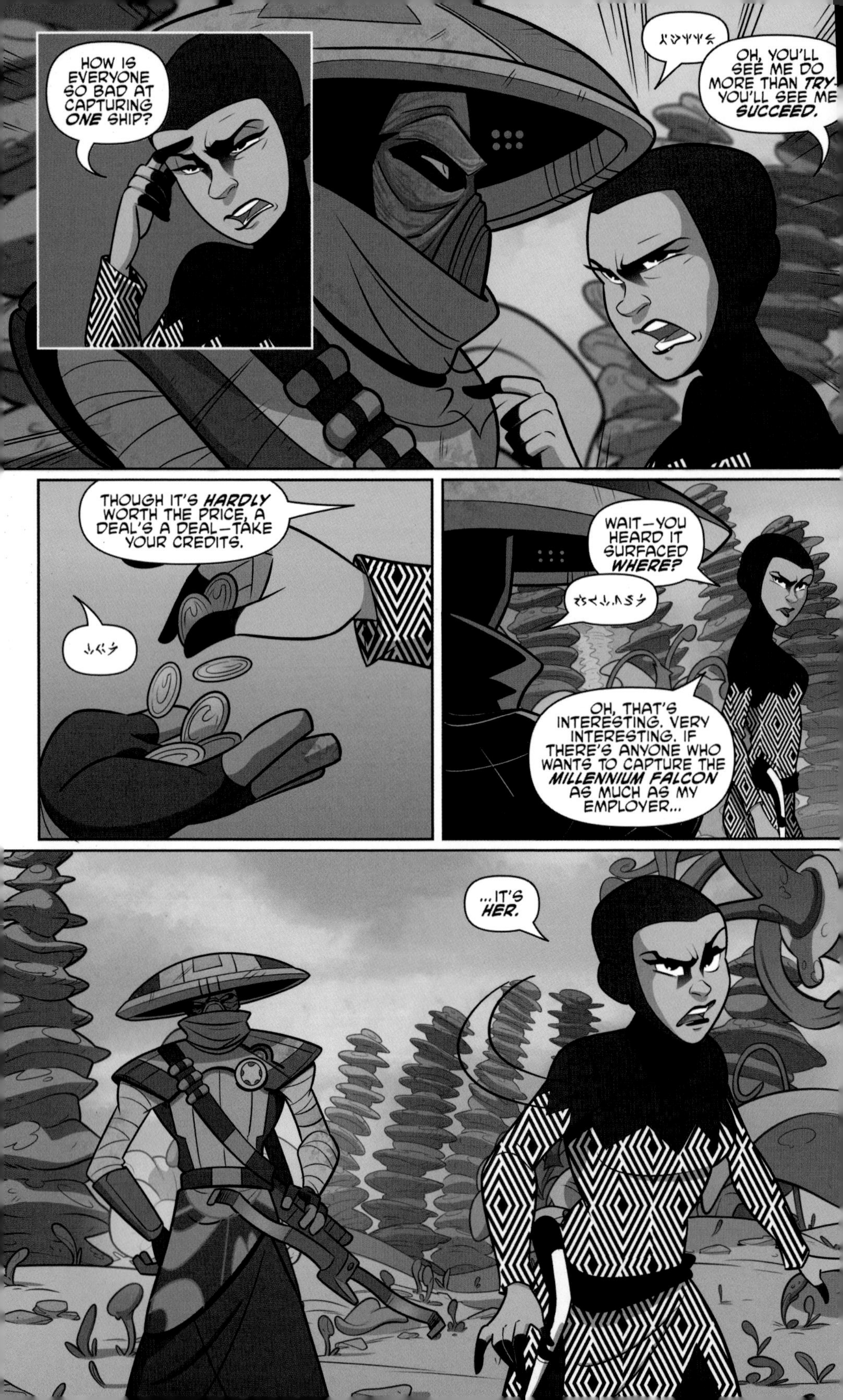
HOW IS EVERYONE SO BAD AT CAPTURING *ONE* SHIP?
OH, YOU'LL SEE ME DO MORE THAN *TRY*— YOU'LL SEE ME *SUCCEED.*
THOUGH IT'S *HARDLY* WORTH THE PRICE, A DEAL'S A DEAL—TAKE YOUR CREDITS.
WAIT—YOU HEARD IT SURFACED *WHERE?*
OH, THAT'S INTERESTING. VERY INTERESTING. IF THERE'S ANYONE WHO WANTS TO CAPTURE THE *MILLENNIUM FALCON* AS MUCH AS MY EMPLOYER...
...IT'S *HER.*

...WHAT DID YOU SAY THEY'RE CALLING HIM?

SOLO.

AND I'M NOT HERE FOR *HIM*, I'M HERE FOR THE *MILLENNIUM FALCON*.

NOW, UNLESS YOU WANT THINGS TO GET *MESSY*, I SUGGEST YOU TALK.

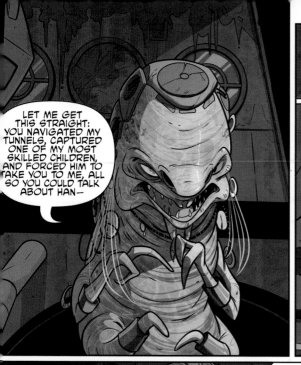

LET ME GET THIS STRAIGHT: YOU NAVIGATED MY TUNNELS, CAPTURED ONE OF MY MOST SKILLED CHILDREN, AND FORCED HIM TO TAKE YOU TO ME, ALL SO YOU COULD TALK ABOUT HAN—

EVEN WHEN HE WAS A KID, I *ALWAYS* KNEW THAT BOY WOULD BE MORE TROUBLE THAN HE WAS WORTH.

DID YOU MISS THE PART WHERE I WAS THREATENING YOU AND YOUR FRIEND WITH A BLASTER?

RELAX. IF YOU WANTED HELP GRINDING HAN'S BELOVED SHIP INTO SPACE DUST...

...ALL YOU HAD TO DO WAS *ASK*.

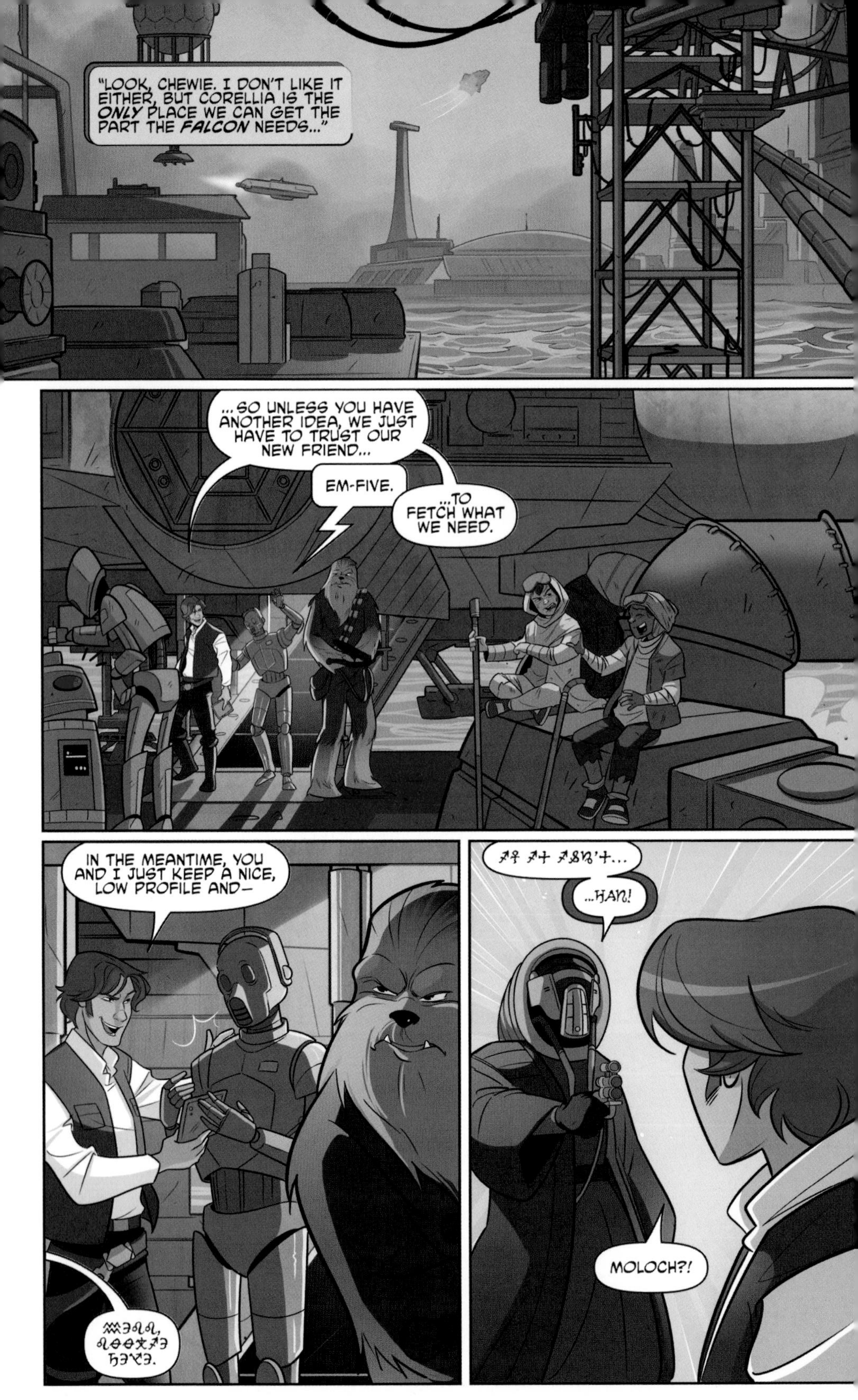
"LOOK, CHEWIE. I DON'T LIKE IT EITHER, BUT CORELLIA IS THE *ONLY* PLACE WE CAN GET THE PART THE *FALCON* NEEDS..."
...SO UNLESS YOU HAVE ANOTHER IDEA, WE JUST HAVE TO TRUST OUR NEW FRIEND...
EM-FIVE.
...TO FETCH WHAT WE NEED.
IN THE MEANTIME, YOU AND I JUST KEEP A NICE, LOW PROFILE AND—
...HAN!
MOLOCH?!

HOW DID YOU KNOW I WAS EVEN HERE?!

DON'T TELL ME YOU'VE JUST BEEN *WAITING* FOR ME SINCE I LEFT THIS PLACE.

ᐯᖉᗝᙢᓰᙢᗩ ᙏᗩᖉᎢᔑ Ꭲᗝ ᔑᎦᎦ Ꭹᗝᘉ.

OH, I BET LADY PROXIMA *HAS* BEEN WANTING TO SEE ME.

BUT YOU SEE, MY FRIEND AND I ARE ON A *BIT* OF A TIGHT SCHEDULE, SO—

ᎦᗩᘉᗷᎩᔑ!

WELL, HOLD ON—JUST *HOLD ON.*

WHAT I MEANT IS THAT BECAUSE MY FRIEND AND I ARE ON SUCH A TIGHT SCHEDULE...

...WE'D BETTER GO AND SEE PROXIMA *RIGHT* AWAY.

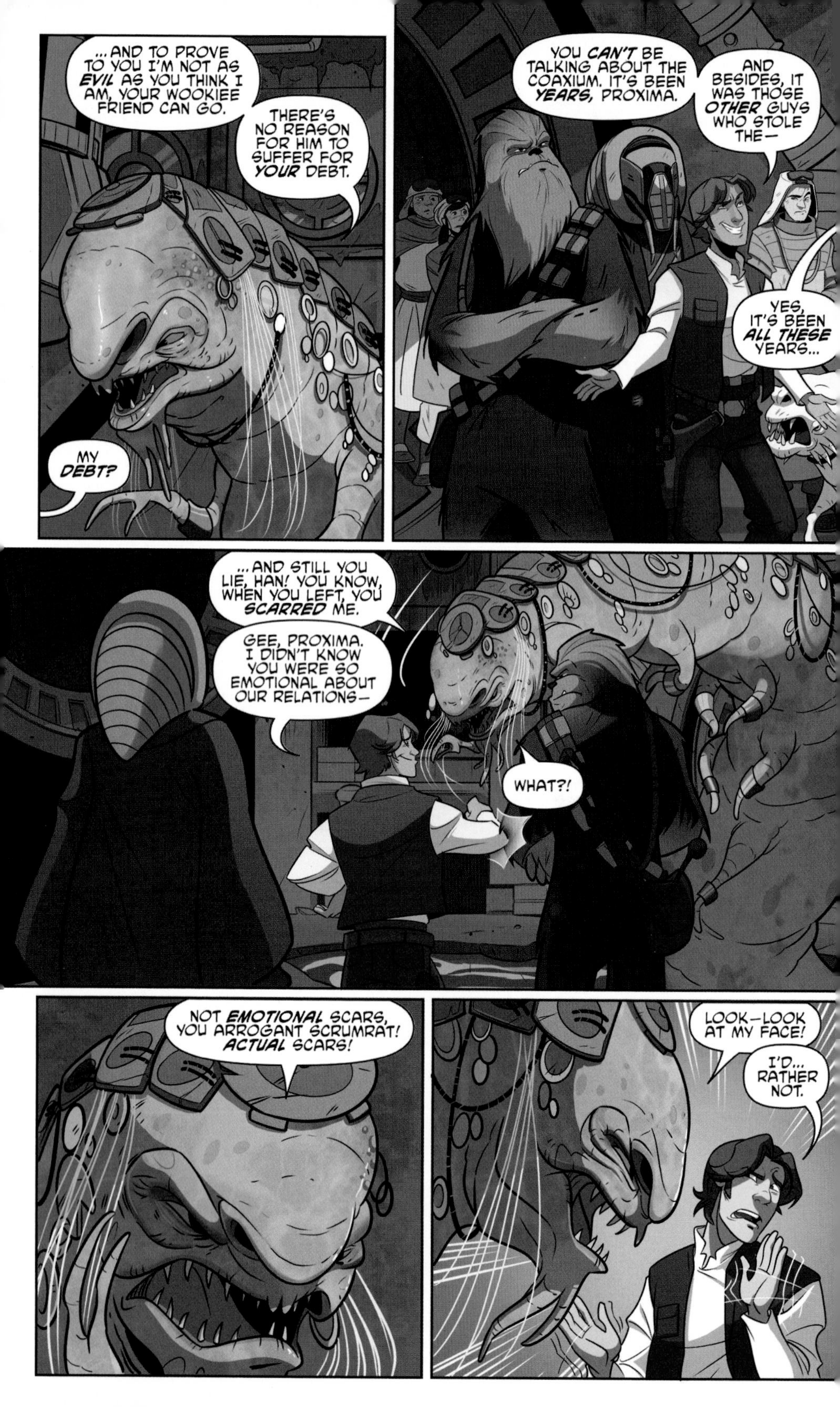

...AND TO PROVE TO YOU I'M NOT AS EVIL AS YOU THINK I AM, YOUR WOOKIEE FRIEND CAN GO.
THERE'S NO REASON FOR HIM TO SUFFER FOR YOUR DEBT.
MY DEBT?
YOU CAN'T BE TALKING ABOUT THE COAXIUM. IT'S BEEN YEARS, PROXIMA.
AND BESIDES, IT WAS THOSE OTHER GUYS WHO STOLE THE—
YES, IT'S BEEN ALL THESE YEARS...
...AND STILL YOU LIE, HAN! YOU KNOW, WHEN YOU LEFT, YOU SCARRED ME.
GEE, PROXIMA. I DIDN'T KNOW YOU WERE SO EMOTIONAL ABOUT OUR RELATIONS—
WHAT?!
NOT EMOTIONAL SCARS, YOU ARROGANT SCRUMRAT! ACTUAL SCARS!
LOOK—LOOK AT MY FACE!
I'D... RATHER NOT.

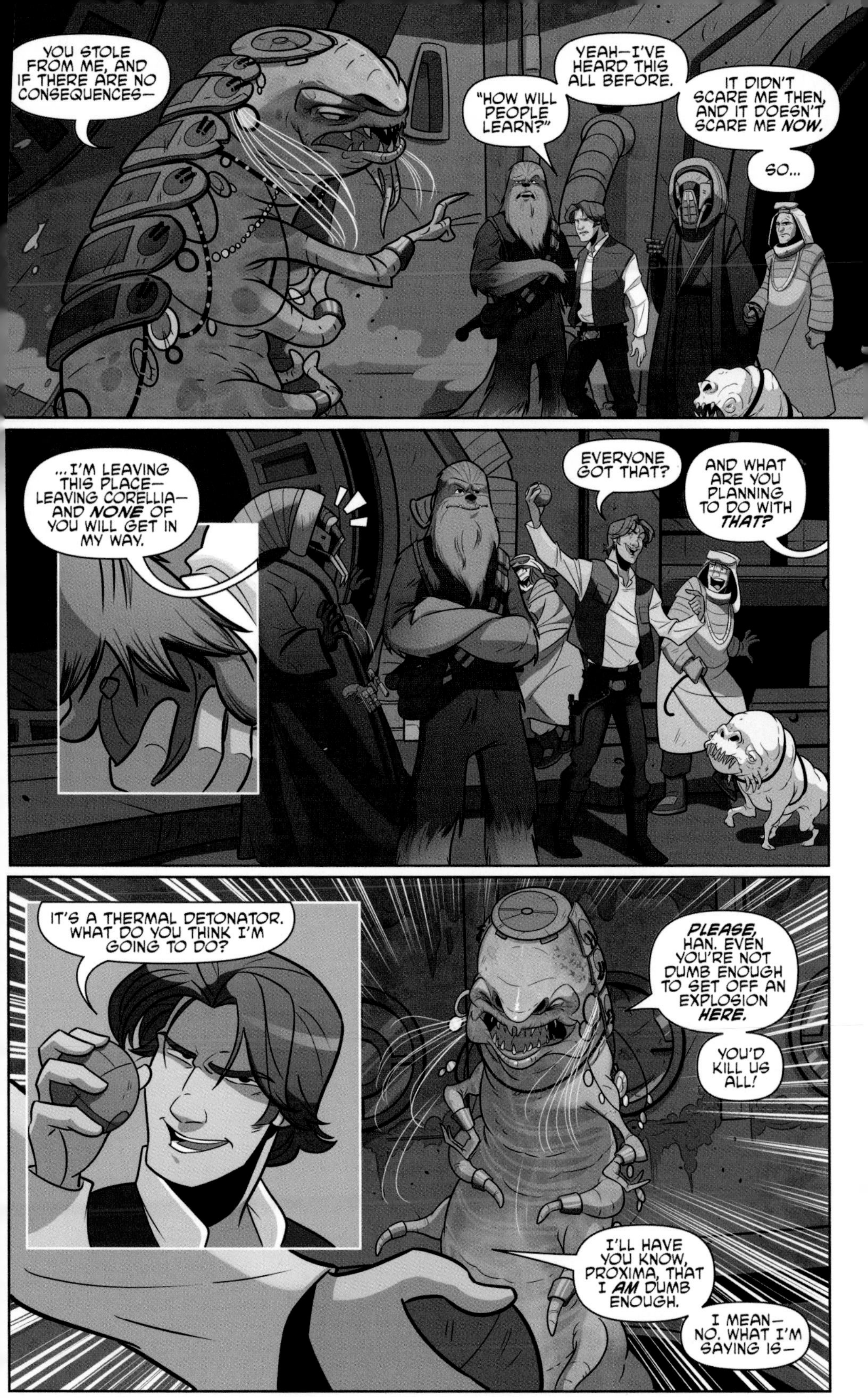
YOU STOLE FROM ME, AND IF THERE ARE NO CONSEQUENCES—
"HOW WILL PEOPLE LEARN?"
YEAH—I'VE HEARD THIS ALL BEFORE.
IT DIDN'T SCARE ME THEN, AND IT DOESN'T SCARE ME *NOW.*
SO...
...I'M LEAVING THIS PLACE— LEAVING CORELLIA— AND ***NONE*** OF YOU WILL GET IN MY WAY.
EVERYONE GOT THAT?
AND WHAT ARE YOU PLANNING TO DO WITH ***THAT?***
IT'S A THERMAL DETONATOR. WHAT DO YOU THINK I'M GOING TO DO?
PLEASE, HAN. EVEN YOU'RE NOT DUMB ENOUGH TO SET OFF AN EXPLOSION ***HERE.***
YOU'D KILL US ALL!
I'LL HAVE YOU KNOW, PROXIMA, THAT I ***AM*** DUMB ENOUGH.
I MEAN— NO. WHAT I'M SAYING IS—

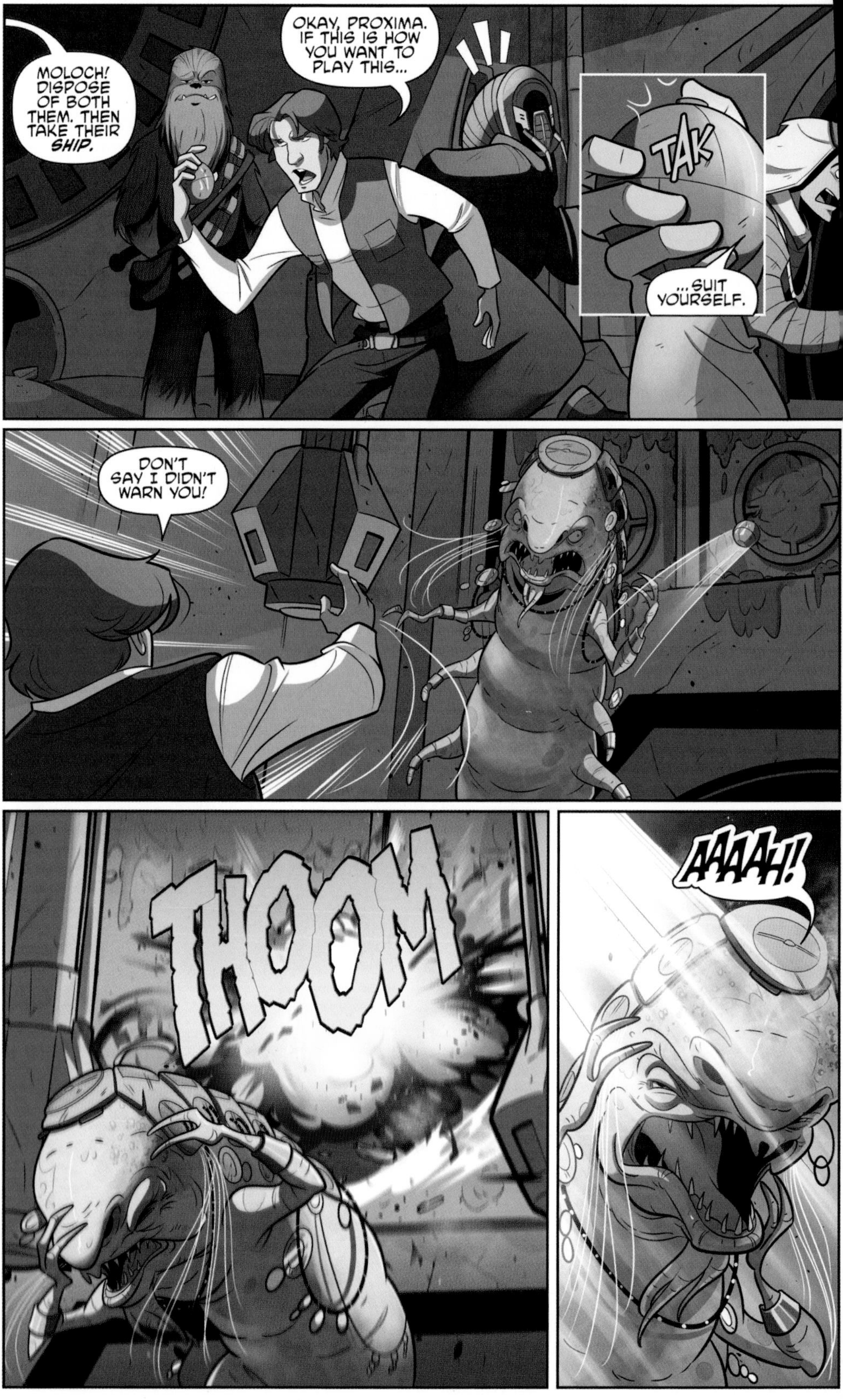
MOLOCH! DISPOSE OF BOTH THEM. THEN TAKE THEIR SHIP.
OKAY, PROXIMA. IF THIS IS HOW YOU WANT TO PLAY THIS...
TAK
...SUIT YOURSELF.
DON'T SAY I DIDN'T WARN YOU!
THOOM
AAAAH!

MRRAAW!

OF COURSE I KNEW WHAT I WAS DOING! I *ALWAYS* HAVE A PLAN... EVEN IF I DON'T KNOW WHAT IT IS.

AND HEY, EVERYTHING TURNED OUT JUST FI—

AAAH!

FZZT

†A⌐Ǝ †�5A†, 5A⌐!

DO YOU KNOW PEOPLE ARE SHOOTING AT YOU?

WHAT ELSE IS NEW?!

I SEE. WELL, YOUR PART IS SECURE, AND YOU CAN FLY.

I CAN FLY.

THAT'S THE ONLY THING I'VE EVER WANTED.

COME ON, CHEWIE...

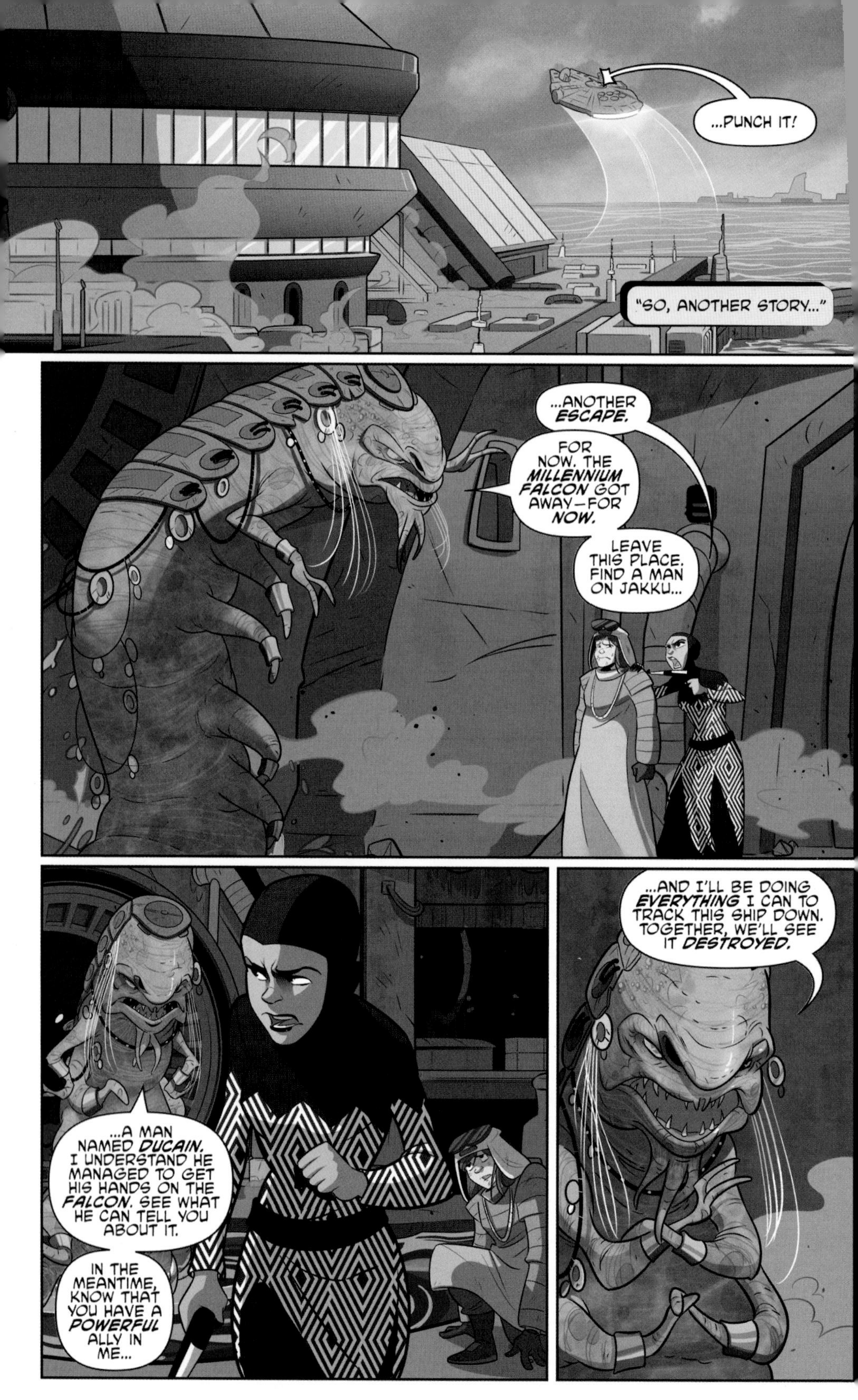
...PUNCH IT!
"SO, ANOTHER STORY..."
...ANOTHER ESCAPE.
FOR NOW. THE MILLENNIUM FALCON GOT AWAY—FOR NOW.
LEAVE THIS PLACE. FIND A MAN ON JAKKU...
...A MAN NAMED DUCAIN. I UNDERSTAND HE MANAGED TO GET HIS HANDS ON THE FALCON. SEE WHAT HE CAN TELL YOU ABOUT IT.
IN THE MEANTIME, KNOW THAT YOU HAVE A POWERFUL ALLY IN ME...
...AND I'LL BE DOING EVERYTHING I CAN TO TRACK THIS SHIP DOWN. TOGETHER, WE'LL SEE IT DESTROYED.

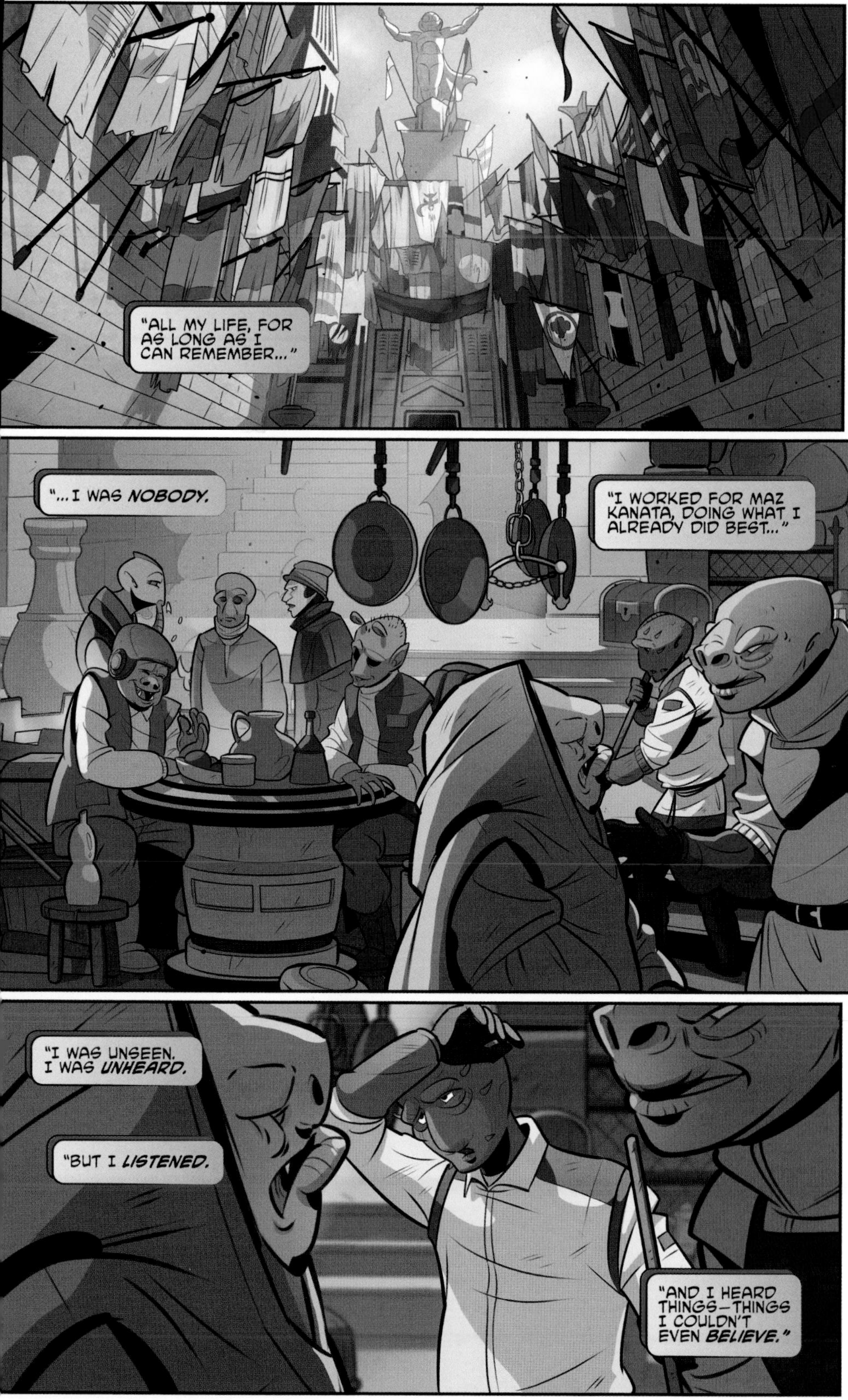
"ALL MY LIFE, FOR AS LONG AS I CAN REMEMBER..."
"...I WAS NOBODY.
"I WORKED FOR MAZ KANATA, DOING WHAT I ALREADY DID BEST..."
"I WAS UNSEEN. I WAS UNHEARD.
"BUT I LISTENED.
"AND I HEARD THINGS—THINGS I COULDN'T EVEN BELIEVE."

"THESE SMUGGLERS AND PIRATES, THEY LIVED LIVES THAT FELT SO... *BIG* TO ME."

... THERE I WAS ON' NAR SHADDAA, AND THAT HUTT WAS ABOUT TO DOUBLE-CROSS ME.

BUT I *EXPECTED* THAT, AND I HAD MY CREW IN POSITION WHEN...

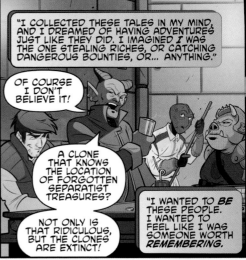

"I COLLECTED THESE TALES IN MY MIND, AND I DREAMED OF HAVING ADVENTURES JUST LIKE THEY DID. I IMAGINED *I* WAS THE ONE STEALING RICHES, OR CATCHING DANGEROUS BOUNTIES, OR... ANYTHING."

OF COURSE I DON'T BELIEVE IT!

A CLONE THAT KNOWS THE LOCATION OF FORGOTTEN SEPARATIST TREASURES?

NOT ONLY IS THAT RIDICULOUS, BUT THE CLONES ARE EXTINCT!

"I WANTED TO *BE* THESE PEOPLE. I WANTED TO FEEL LIKE I WAS SOMEONE WORTH *REMEMBERING*.

"AND THEN, ONE DAY..."

LOOK, I KNOW THE WOOKIEE TREE THING IS IMPORTANT TO CHEWIE. I'M JUST SAYING THINGS WOULD BE EASIER IF HE WAS AROUND.

CHEWIE'S WITH HIS *FAMILY*. MAYBE THAT'S SOMETHING YOU OUGHT TO THINK ABOUT YOUR-SELF, HMMM?

IT'S JUST A *JOB*, MAZ. I *AM* STILL THE PILOT OF A FREIGHTER, EVEN IF I AM SHORT-HAND—

"...THE GALAXY GAVE ME MY CHANCE."

SHORT-HANDED? I CAN HELP. I CAN BE YOUR CO-PILOT.

AND YOU ARE?

VERY EAGER.

DUCAIN'S A GOOD BOY, HAN. AND YOU COULD USE THE HELP.

FINE. BUT YOU'RE HERE TO *WORK*. IF YOU THINK YOU'RE COMING ALONG FOR SOME JOYRIDE...

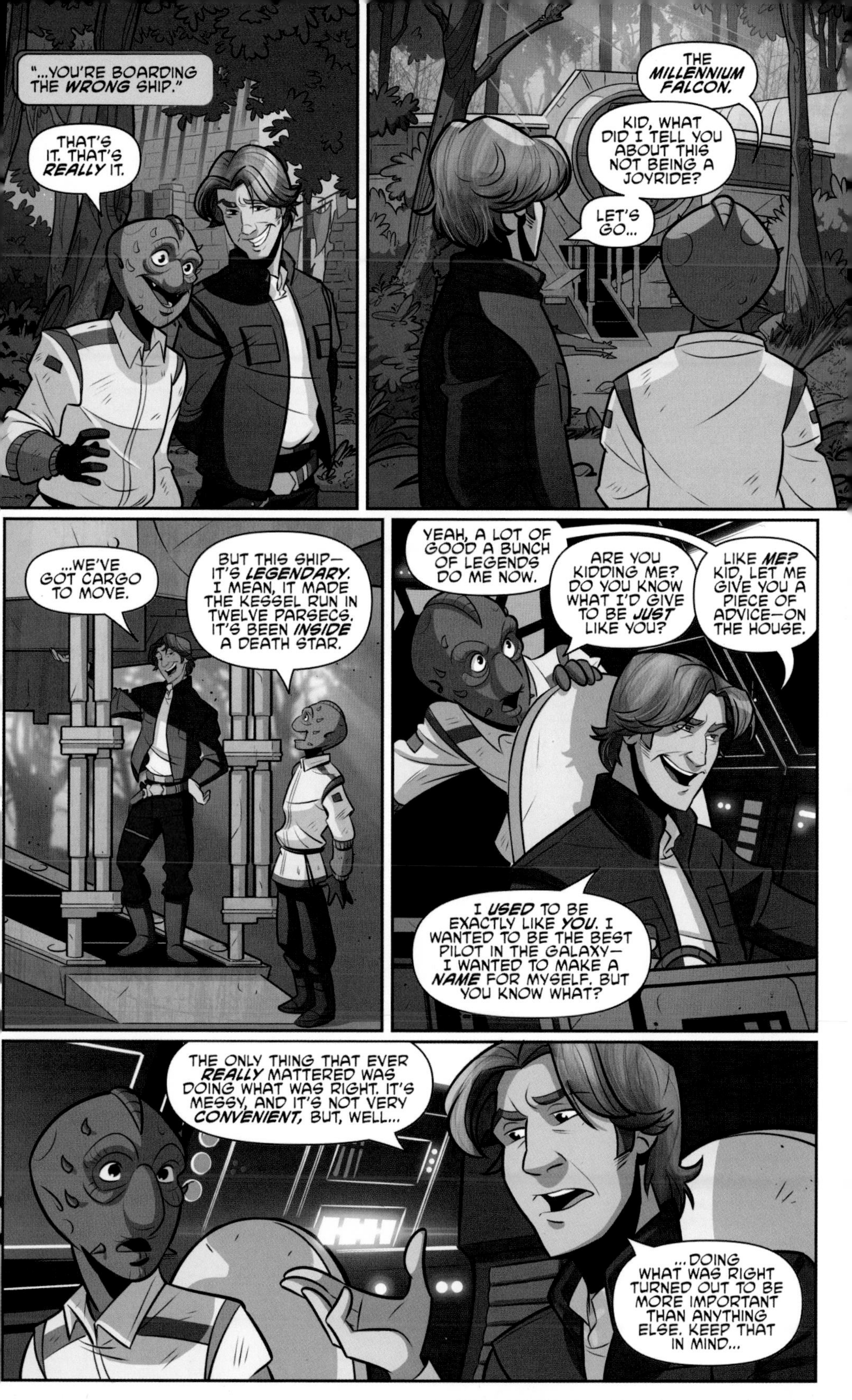
"...YOU'RE BOARDING THE WRONG SHIP."
THAT'S IT. THAT'S REALLY IT.
THE MILLENNIUM FALCON.
KID, WHAT DID I TELL YOU ABOUT THIS NOT BEING A JOYRIDE?
LET'S GO...
...WE'VE GOT CARGO TO MOVE.
BUT THIS SHIP— IT'S LEGENDARY. I MEAN, IT MADE THE KESSEL RUN IN TWELVE PARSECS. IT'S BEEN INSIDE A DEATH STAR.
YEAH, A LOT OF GOOD A BUNCH OF LEGENDS DO ME NOW.
ARE YOU KIDDING ME? DO YOU KNOW WHAT I'D GIVE TO BE JUST LIKE YOU?
LIKE ME? KID, LET ME GIVE YOU A PIECE OF ADVICE—ON THE HOUSE.
I USED TO BE EXACTLY LIKE YOU. I WANTED TO BE THE BEST PILOT IN THE GALAXY— I WANTED TO MAKE A NAME FOR MYSELF. BUT YOU KNOW WHAT?
THE ONLY THING THAT EVER REALLY MATTERED WAS DOING WHAT WAS RIGHT. IT'S MESSY, AND IT'S NOT VERY CONVENIENT, BUT, WELL...
...DOING WHAT WAS RIGHT TURNED OUT TO BE MORE IMPORTANT THAN ANYTHING ELSE. KEEP THAT IN MIND...

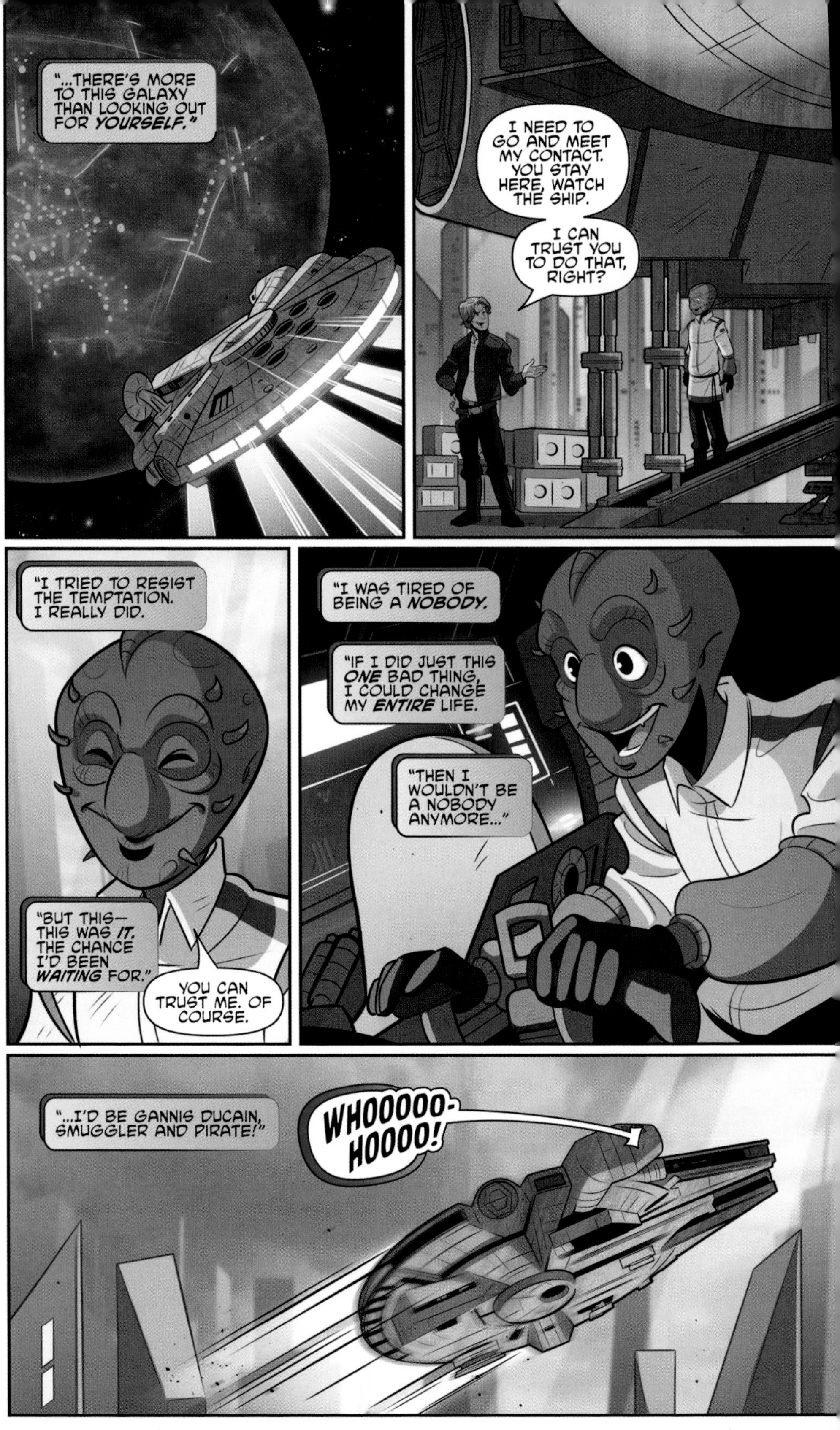
"...THERE'S MORE TO THIS GALAXY THAN LOOKING OUT FOR *YOURSELF.*"
I NEED TO GO AND MEET MY CONTACT. YOU STAY HERE, WATCH THE SHIP.
I CAN TRUST YOU TO DO THAT, RIGHT?
"I TRIED TO RESIST THE TEMPTATION. I REALLY DID.
"BUT THIS— THIS WAS *IT.* THE CHANCE I'D BEEN *WAITING* FOR."
YOU CAN TRUST ME. OF COURSE.
"I WAS TIRED OF BEING A *NOBODY.*
"IF I DID JUST THIS *ONE* BAD THING, I COULD CHANGE MY *ENTIRE* LIFE.
"THEN I WOULDN'T BE A NOBODY ANYMORE..."
"...I'D BE GANNIS DUCAIN, SMUGGLER AND PIRATE!"
WHOOOOO-HOOOO!

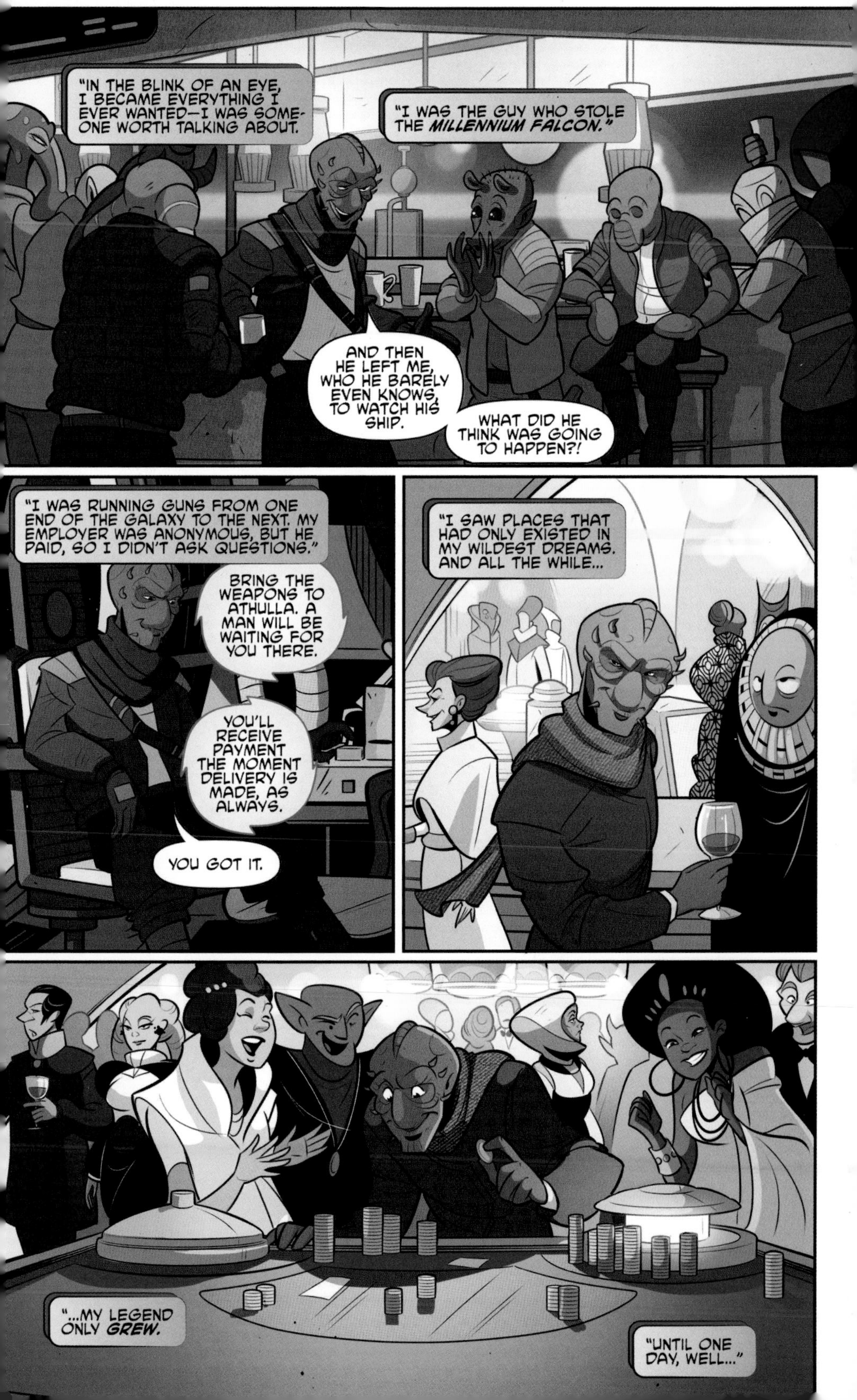

"IN THE BLINK OF AN EYE, I BECAME EVERYTHING I EVER WANTED—I WAS SOME-ONE WORTH TALKING ABOUT.
"I WAS THE GUY WHO STOLE THE *MILLENNIUM FALCON.*"
AND THEN HE LEFT ME, WHO HE BARELY EVEN KNOWS, TO WATCH HIS SHIP.
WHAT DID HE THINK WAS GOING TO HAPPEN?!
"I WAS RUNNING GUNS FROM ONE END OF THE GALAXY TO THE NEXT. MY EMPLOYER WAS ANONYMOUS, BUT HE PAID, SO I DIDN'T ASK QUESTIONS."
BRING THE WEAPONS TO ATHULLA. A MAN WILL BE WAITING FOR YOU THERE.
YOU'LL RECEIVE PAYMENT THE MOMENT DELIVERY IS MADE, AS ALWAYS.
YOU GOT IT.
"I SAW PLACES THAT HAD ONLY EXISTED IN MY WILDEST DREAMS. AND ALL THE WHILE...
"...MY LEGEND ONLY *GREW.*
"UNTIL ONE DAY, WELL..."

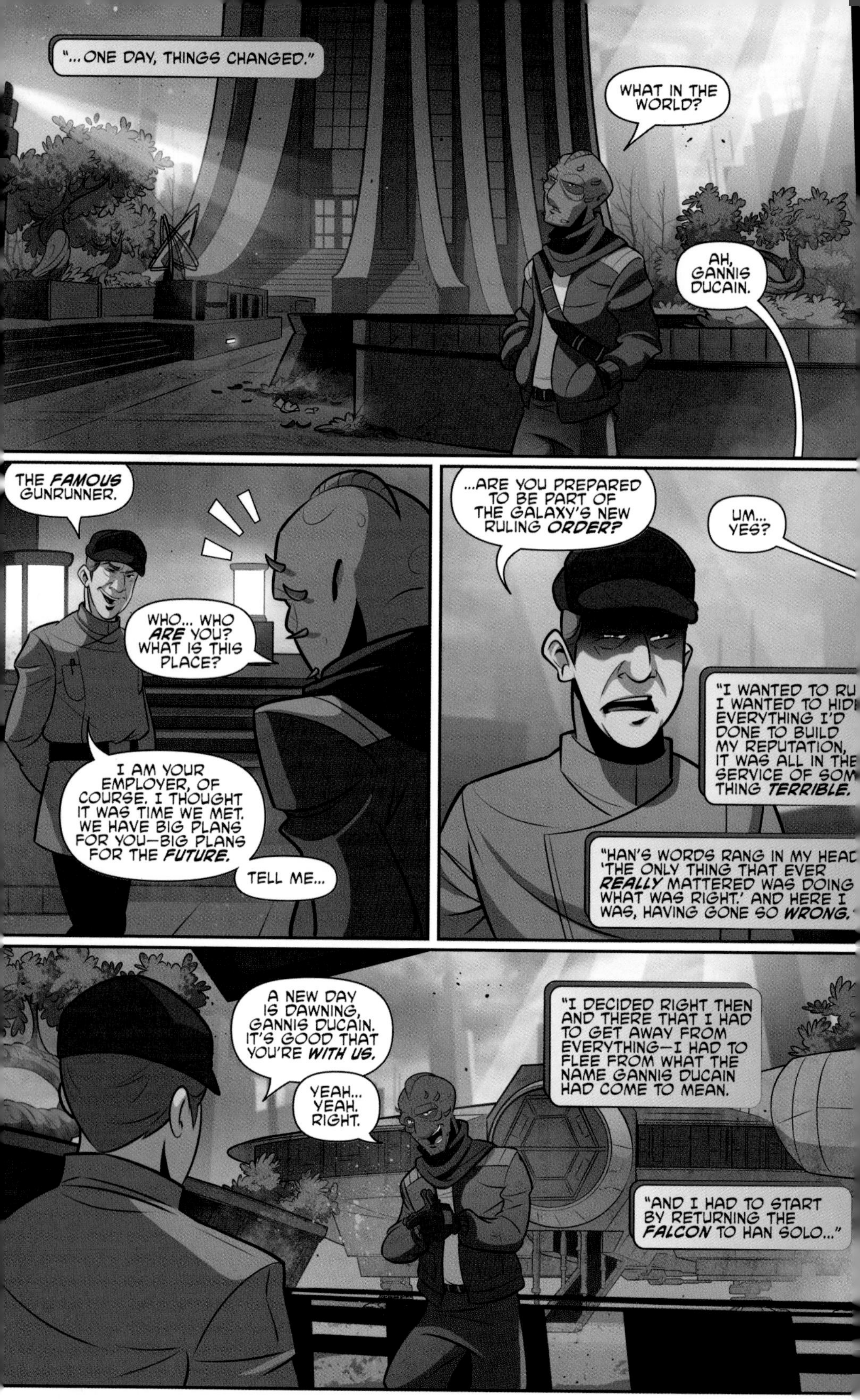
"...ONE DAY, THINGS CHANGED."
WHAT IN THE WORLD?
AH, GANNIS DUCAIN.
THE FAMOUS GUNRUNNER.
WHO... WHO ARE YOU? WHAT IS THIS PLACE?
I AM YOUR EMPLOYER, OF COURSE. I THOUGHT IT WAS TIME WE MET. WE HAVE BIG PLANS FOR YOU—BIG PLANS FOR THE FUTURE.
TELL ME...
...ARE YOU PREPARED TO BE PART OF THE GALAXY'S NEW RULING ORDER?
UM... YES?
"I WANTED TO RU I WANTED TO HID EVERYTHING I'D DONE TO BUILD MY REPUTATION, IT WAS ALL IN THE SERVICE OF SOM THING TERRIBLE.
"HAN'S WORDS RANG IN MY HEAD 'THE ONLY THING THAT EVER REALLY MATTERED WAS DOING WHAT WAS RIGHT.' AND HERE I WAS, HAVING GONE SO WRONG.
A NEW DAY IS DAWNING, GANNIS DUCAIN. IT'S GOOD THAT YOU'RE WITH US.
YEAH... YEAH. RIGHT.
"I DECIDED RIGHT THEN AND THERE THAT I HAD TO GET AWAY FROM EVERYTHING—I HAD TO FLEE FROM WHAT THE NAME GANNIS DUCAIN HAD COME TO MEAN.
"AND I HAD TO START BY RETURNING THE FALCON TO HAN SOLO..."

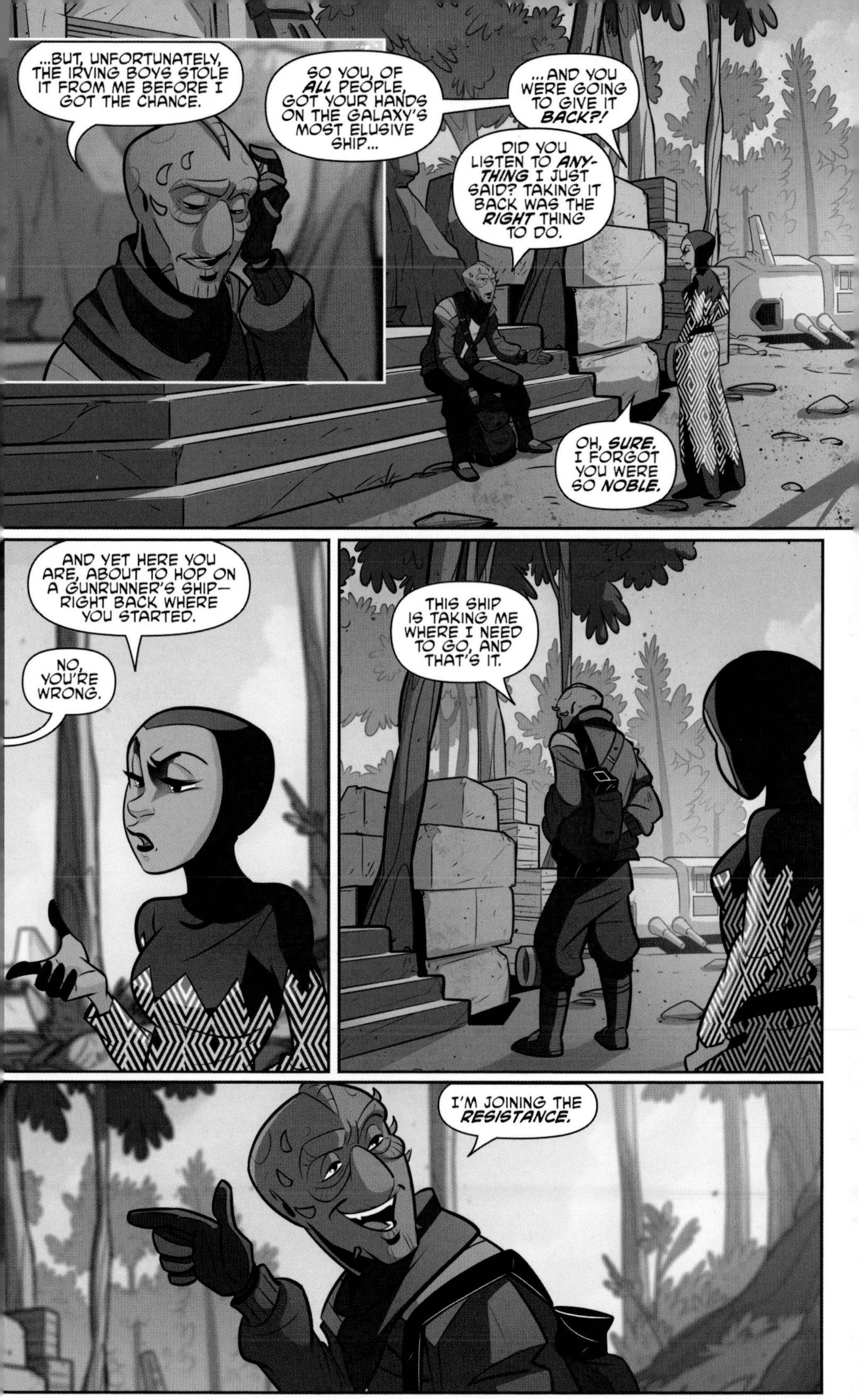
...BUT, UNFORTUNATELY, THE IRVING BOYS STOLE IT FROM ME BEFORE I GOT THE CHANCE.
SO YOU, OF ALL PEOPLE, GOT YOUR HANDS ON THE GALAXY'S MOST ELUSIVE SHIP...
...AND YOU WERE GOING TO GIVE IT BACK?!
DID YOU LISTEN TO ANYTHING I JUST SAID? TAKING IT BACK WAS THE RIGHT THING TO DO.
OH, SURE. I FORGOT YOU WERE SO NOBLE.
AND YET HERE YOU ARE, ABOUT TO HOP ON A GUNRUNNER'S SHIP—RIGHT BACK WHERE YOU STARTED.
NO, YOU'RE WRONG.
THIS SHIP IS TAKING ME WHERE I NEED TO GO, AND THAT'S IT.
I'M JOINING THE RESISTANCE.

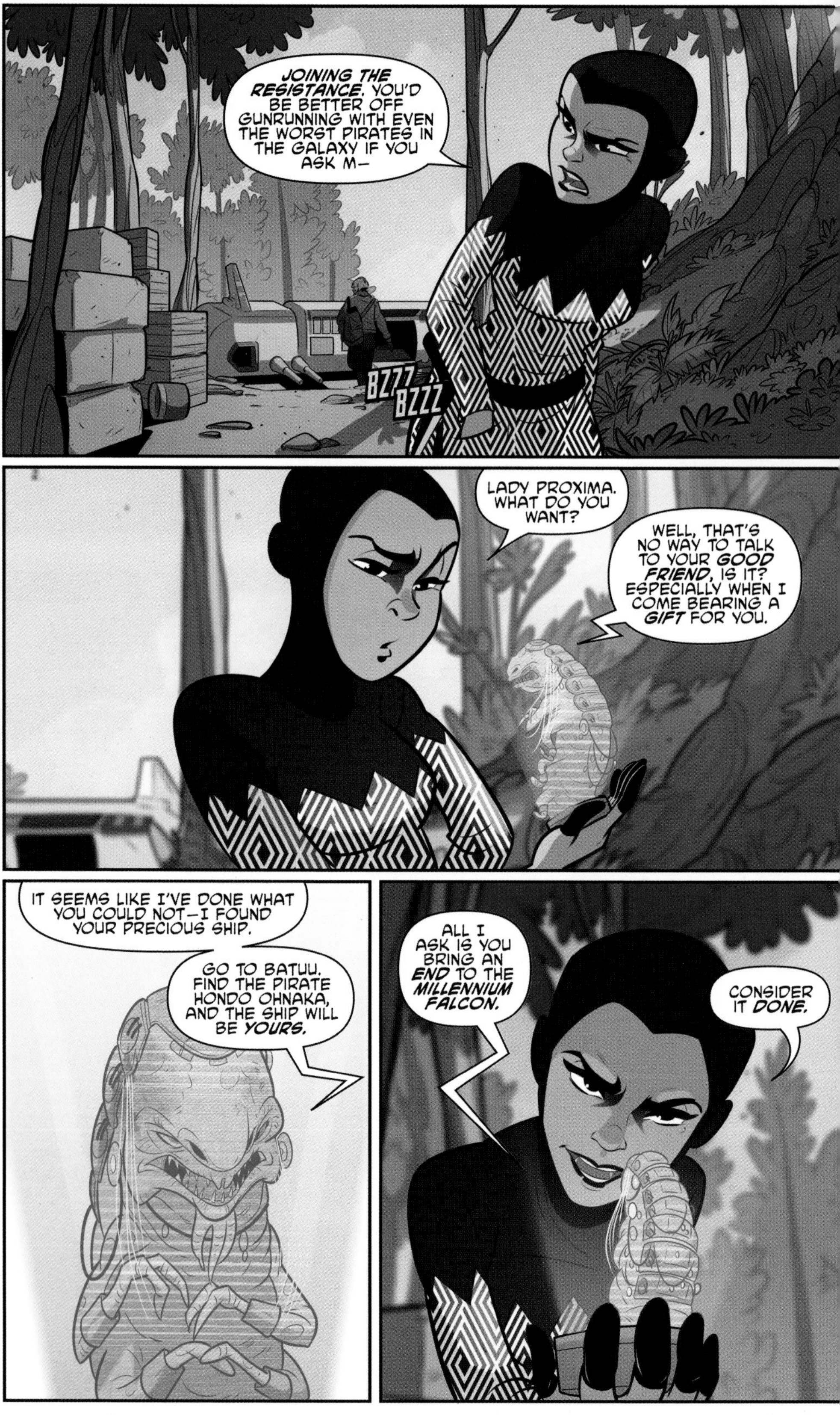
JOINING THE RESISTANCE. YOU'D BE BETTER OFF GUNRUNNING WITH EVEN THE WORST PIRATES IN THE GALAXY IF YOU ASK M—
BZZZ BZZZ
LADY PROXIMA. WHAT DO YOU WANT?
WELL, THAT'S NO WAY TO TALK TO YOUR GOOD FRIEND, IS IT? ESPECIALLY WHEN I COME BEARING A GIFT FOR YOU.
IT SEEMS LIKE I'VE DONE WHAT YOU COULD NOT—I FOUND YOUR PRECIOUS SHIP.
GO TO BATUU. FIND THE PIRATE HONDO OHNAKA, AND THE SHIP WILL BE YOURS.
ALL I ASK IS YOU BRING AN END TO THE MILLENNIUM FALCON.
CONSIDER IT DONE.

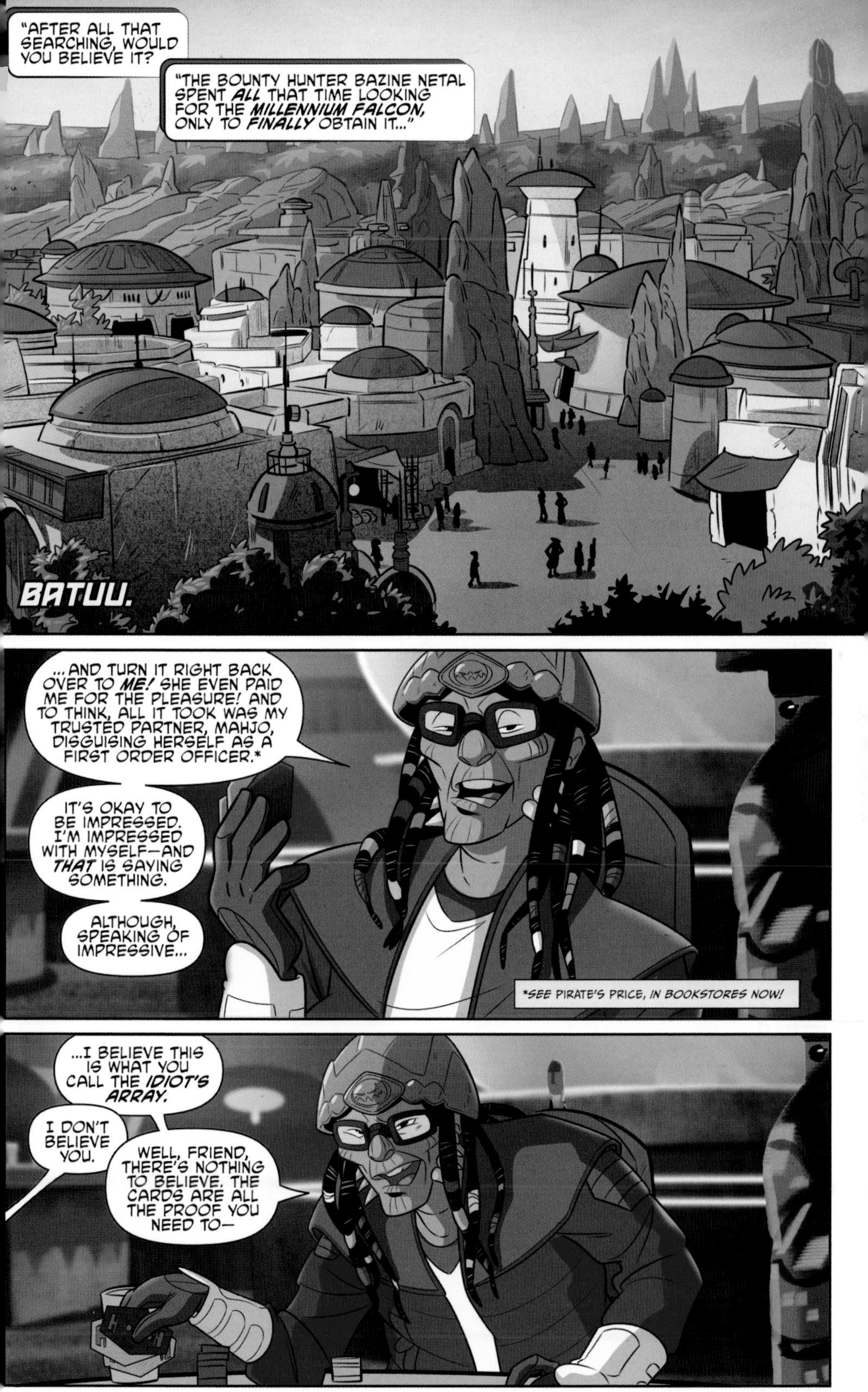
"AFTER ALL THAT SEARCHING, WOULD YOU BELIEVE IT?
"THE BOUNTY HUNTER BAZINE NETAL SPENT ALL THAT TIME LOOKING FOR THE MILLENNIUM FALCON, ONLY TO FINALLY OBTAIN IT..."
BATUU.
...AND TURN IT RIGHT BACK OVER TO ME! SHE EVEN PAID ME FOR THE PLEASURE! AND TO THINK, ALL IT TOOK WAS MY TRUSTED PARTNER, MAHJO, DISGUISING HERSELF AS A FIRST ORDER OFFICER.*
IT'S OKAY TO BE IMPRESSED. I'M IMPRESSED WITH MYSELF—AND THAT IS SAYING SOMETHING.
ALTHOUGH, SPEAKING OF IMPRESSIVE...
*SEE PIRATE'S PRICE, IN BOOKSTORES NOW!
...I BELIEVE THIS IS WHAT YOU CALL THE IDIOT'S ARRAY.
I DON'T BELIEVE YOU.
WELL, FRIEND, THERE'S NOTHING TO BELIEVE. THE CARDS ARE ALL THE PROOF YOU NEED TO—

NOT THE CARDS, PIRATE. I DON'T BELIEVE *YOU* ARE IN POSSESSION OF THE *MILLENNIUM FALCON.*

HOW DARE YOU!

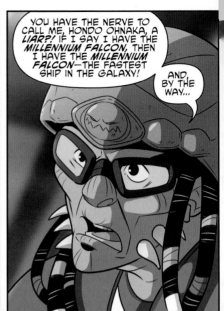
YOU HAVE THE NERVE TO CALL ME, HONDO OHNAKA, A *LIAR?!* IF I SAY I HAVE THE *MILLENNIUM FALCON,* THEN I HAVE THE *MILLENNIUM FALCON*—THE FASTEST SHIP IN THE GALAXY!

AND, BY THE WAY...

...THOSE GUYS IN THE WEIRD RED MASKS—HAVE THEY BEEN WITH YOU THE *ENTIRE* TIME?

TELL ME— IF YOU DO INDEED HAVE THE *FALCON, WHERE* IS IT?

I'LL TELL YOU *EXACTLY* WHERE—

HONDO!

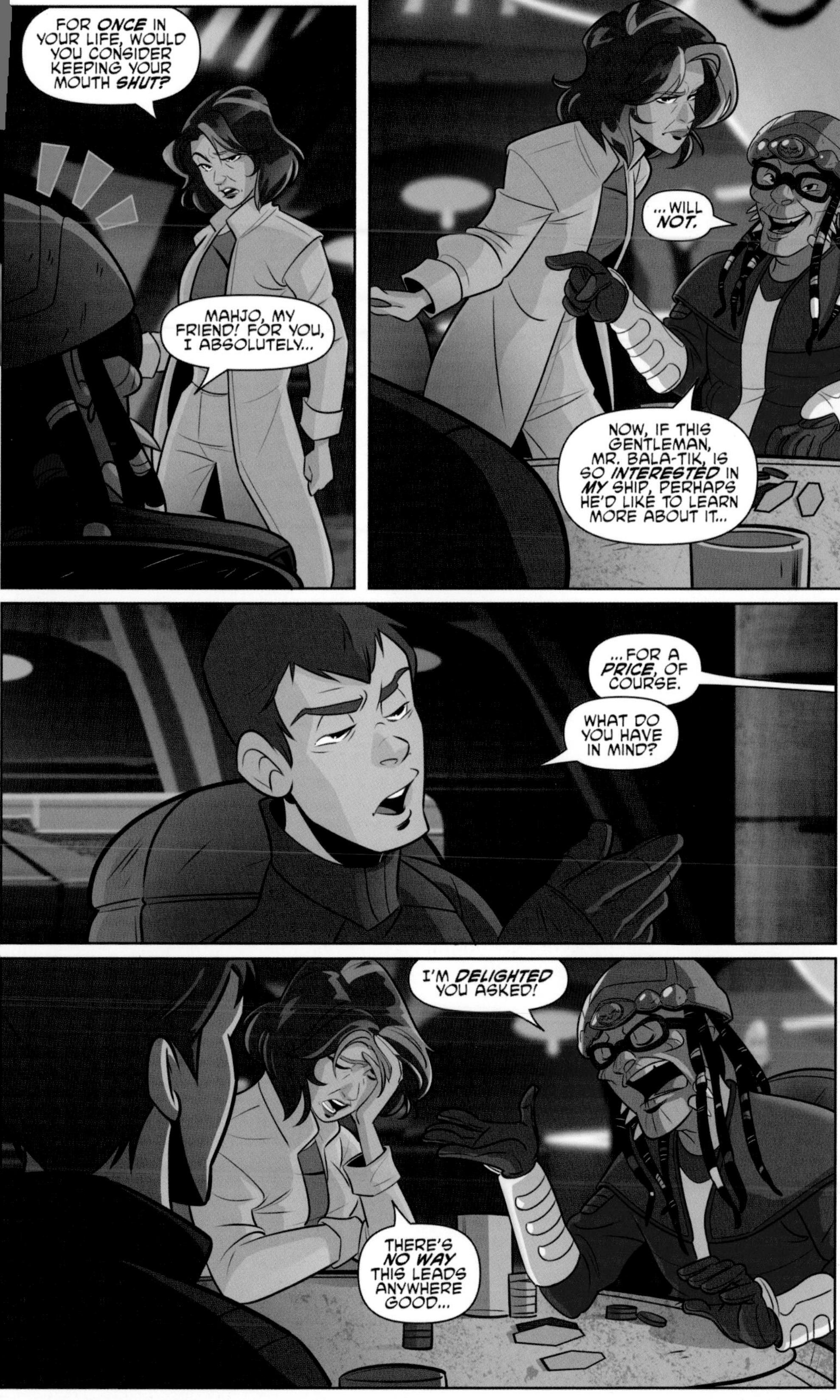
FOR ONCE IN YOUR LIFE, WOULD YOU CONSIDER KEEPING YOUR MOUTH SHUT?
MAHJO, MY FRIEND! FOR YOU, I ABSOLUTELY...
...WILL NOT.
NOW, IF THIS GENTLEMAN, MR. BALA-TIK, IS SO INTERESTED IN MY SHIP, PERHAPS HE'D LIKE TO LEARN MORE ABOUT IT...
...FOR A PRICE, OF COURSE.
WHAT DO YOU HAVE IN MIND?
I'M DELIGHTED YOU ASKED!
THERE'S NO WAY THIS LEADS ANYWHERE GOOD...

NOW, THERE ARE PLENTY OF CORELLIAN FREIGHTERS IN THE GALAXY.

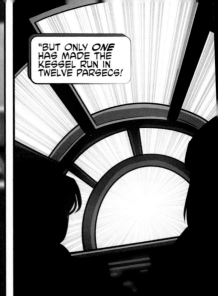

"BUT ONLY *ONE* HAS MADE THE KESSEL RUN IN TWELVE PARSECS!

"ONLY *ONE* HAS DESTROYED THE MIGHTY *DEATH STAR!*

"AND ONLY ONE WAS CAPTAINED BY THE LEGENDARY HAN SOLO!"

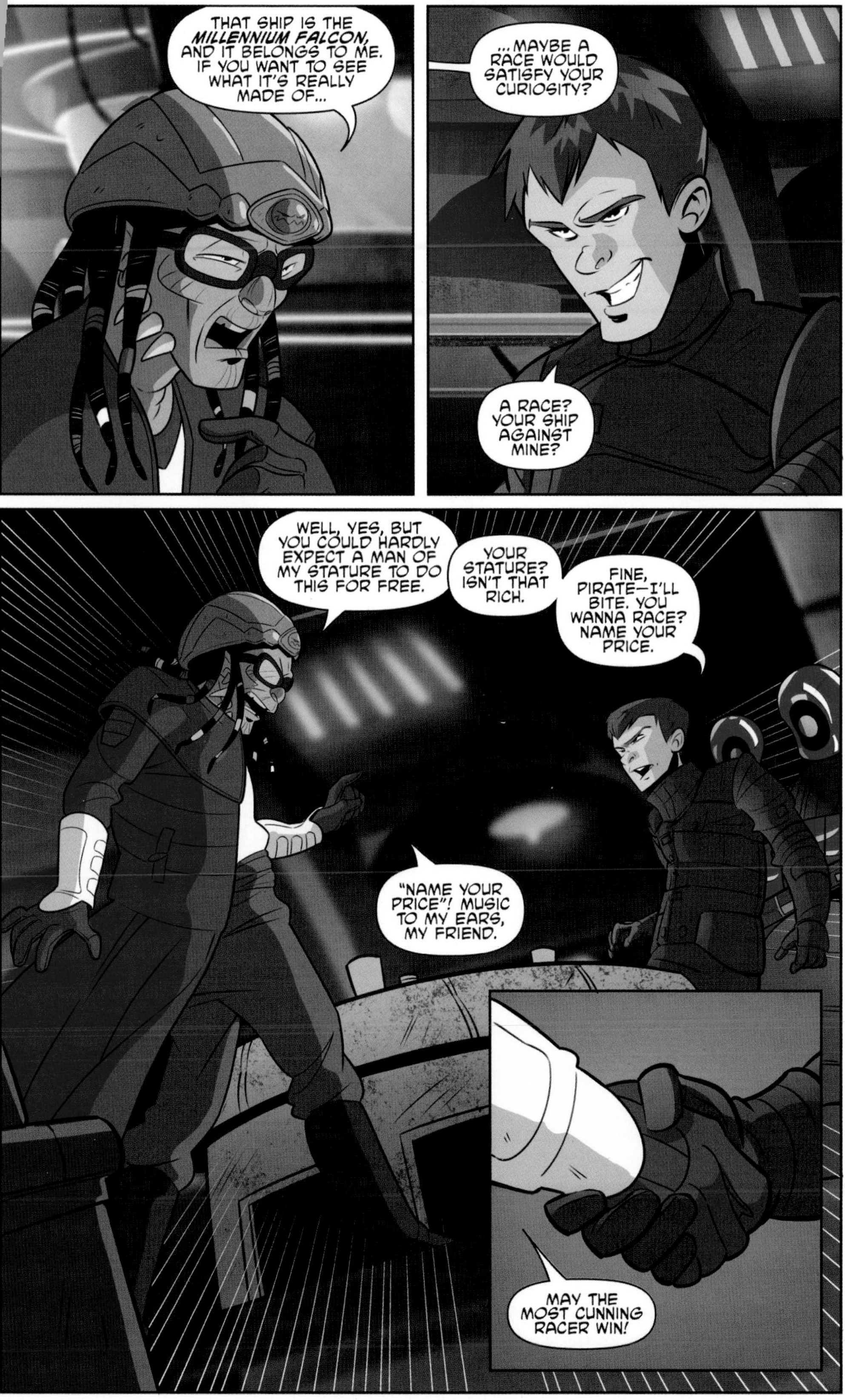
THAT SHIP IS THE *MILLENNIUM FALCON,* AND IT BELONGS TO ME. IF YOU WANT TO SEE WHAT IT'S REALLY MADE OF...
...MAYBE A RACE WOULD SATISFY YOUR CURIOSITY?
A RACE? YOUR SHIP AGAINST MINE?
WELL, YES, BUT YOU COULD HARDLY EXPECT A MAN OF MY STATURE TO DO THIS FOR FREE.
YOUR STATURE? ISN'T THAT RICH.
FINE, PIRATE—I'LL BITE. YOU WANNA RACE? NAME YOUR PRICE.
"NAME YOUR PRICE"! MUSIC TO MY EARS, MY FRIEND.
MAY THE MOST CUNNING RACER WIN!

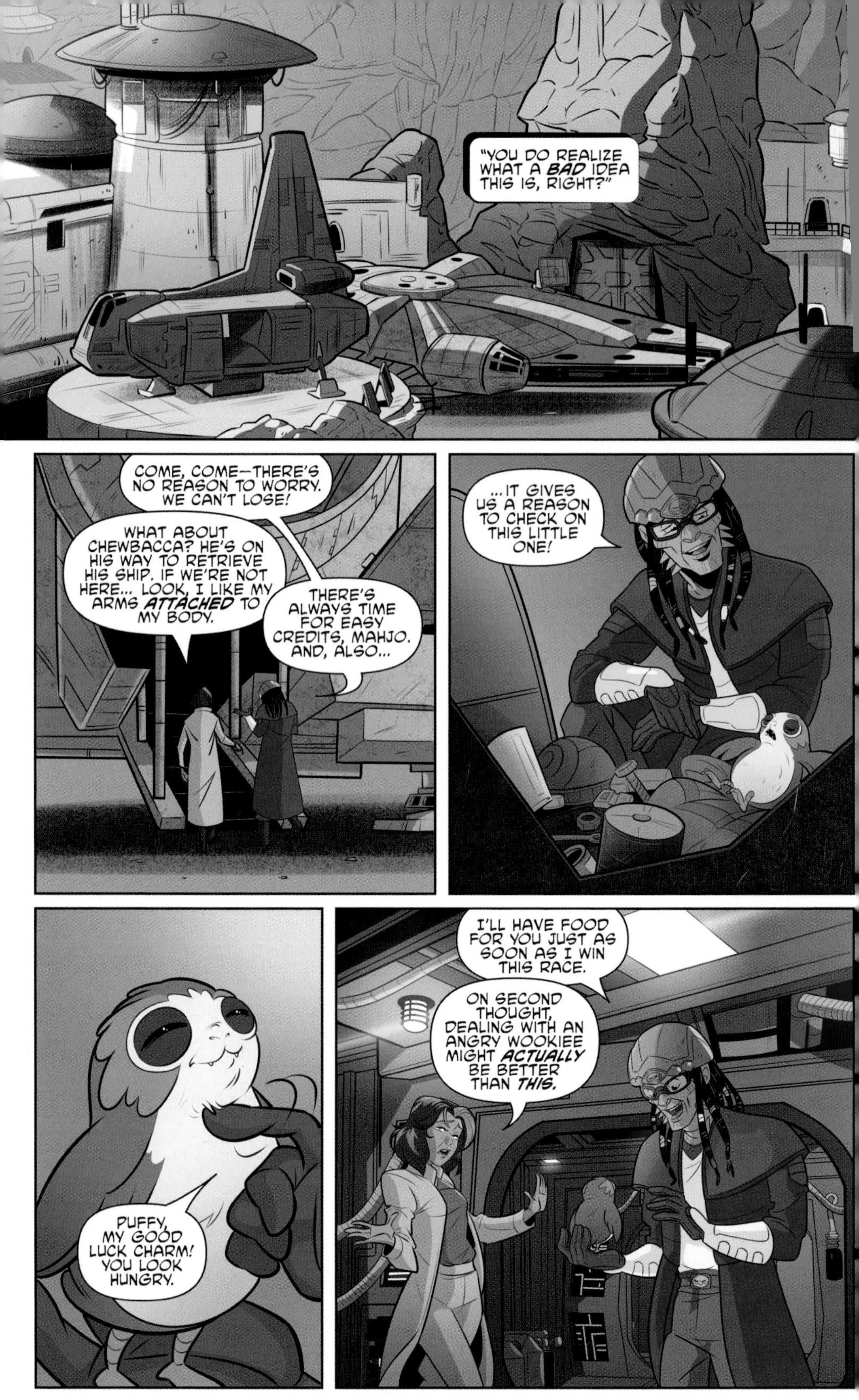
"YOU DO REALIZE WHAT A BAD IDEA THIS IS, RIGHT?"
COME, COME—THERE'S NO REASON TO WORRY. WE CAN'T LOSE!
WHAT ABOUT CHEWBACCA? HE'S ON HIS WAY TO RETRIEVE HIS SHIP. IF WE'RE NOT HERE... LOOK, I LIKE MY ARMS ATTACHED TO MY BODY.
THERE'S ALWAYS TIME FOR EASY CREDITS, MAHJO. AND, ALSO...
...IT GIVES US A REASON TO CHECK ON THIS LITTLE ONE!
PUFFY, MY GOOD LUCK CHARM! YOU LOOK HUNGRY.
I'LL HAVE FOOD FOR YOU JUST AS SOON AS I WIN THIS RACE.
ON SECOND THOUGHT, DEALING WITH AN ANGRY WOOKIEE MIGHT ACTUALLY BE BETTER THAN THIS.

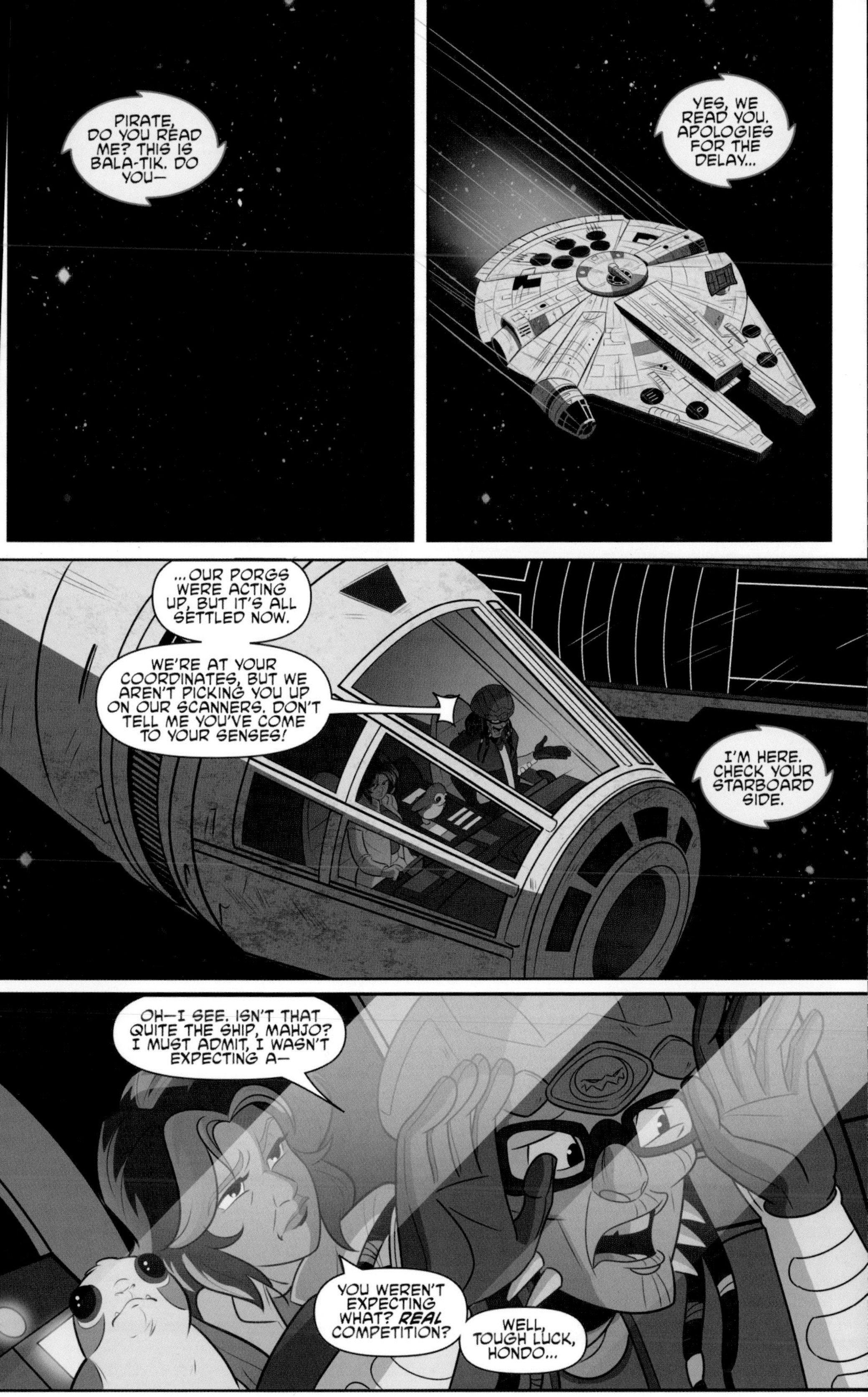
PIRATE, DO YOU READ ME? THIS IS BALA-TIK. DO YOU—
YES, WE READ YOU. APOLOGIES FOR THE DELAY...
...OUR PORGS WERE ACTING UP, BUT IT'S ALL SETTLED NOW.
WE'RE AT YOUR COORDINATES, BUT WE AREN'T PICKING YOU UP ON OUR SCANNERS. DON'T TELL ME YOU'VE COME TO YOUR SENSES!
I'M HERE. CHECK YOUR STARBOARD SIDE.
OH—I SEE. ISN'T THAT QUITE THE SHIP, MAHJO? I MUST ADMIT, I WASN'T EXPECTING A—
YOU WEREN'T EXPECTING WHAT? REAL COMPETITION?
WELL, TOUGH LUCK, HONDO...

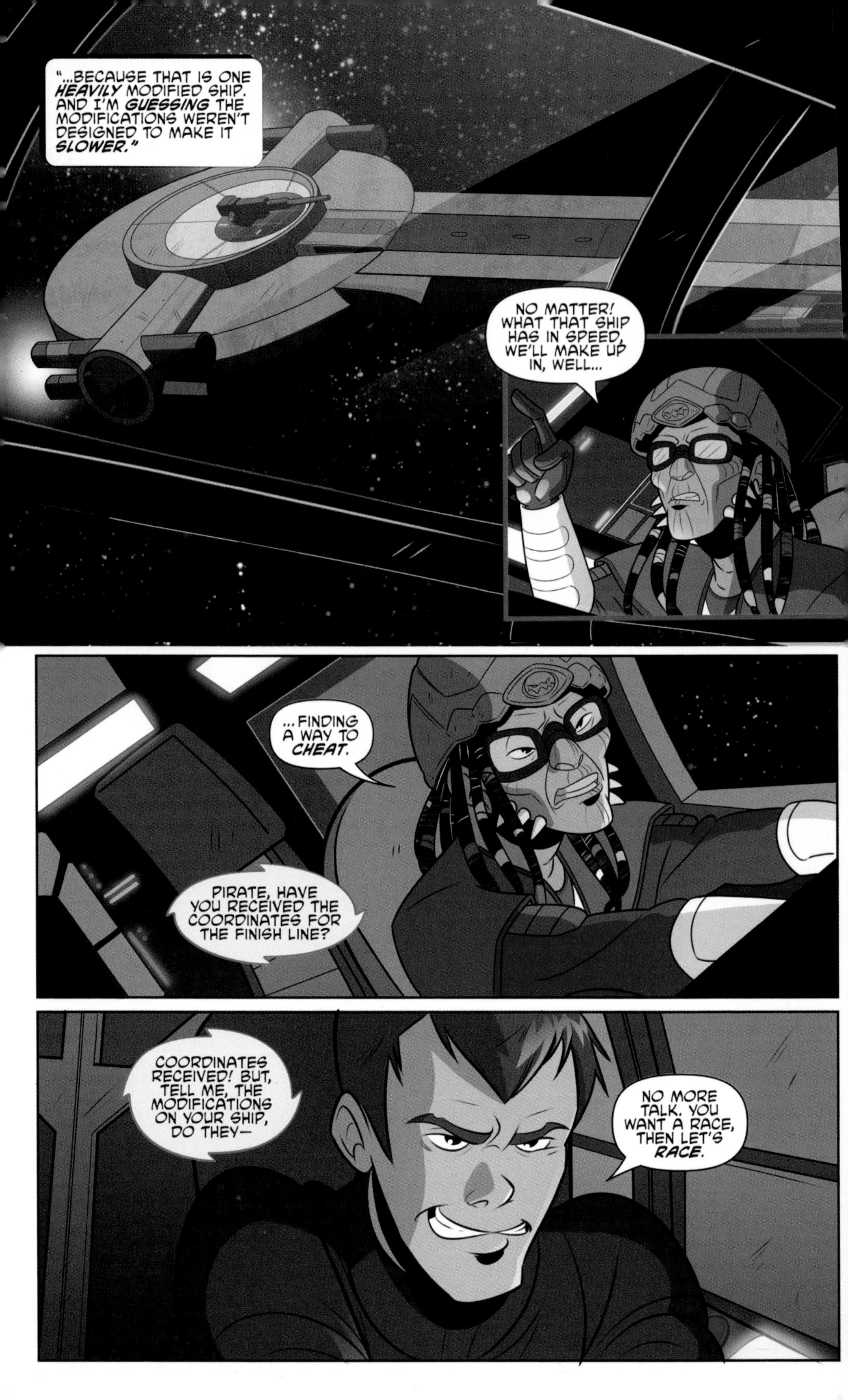
"...BECAUSE THAT IS ONE HEAVILY MODIFIED SHIP. AND I'M GUESSING THE MODIFICATIONS WEREN'T DESIGNED TO MAKE IT SLOWER."
NO MATTER! WHAT THAT SHIP HAS IN SPEED, WE'LL MAKE UP IN, WELL...
...FINDING A WAY TO CHEAT.
PIRATE, HAVE YOU RECEIVED THE COORDINATES FOR THE FINISH LINE?
COORDINATES RECEIVED! BUT, TELL ME, THE MODIFICATIONS ON YOUR SHIP, DO THEY—
NO MORE TALK. YOU WANT A RACE, THEN LET'S RACE.

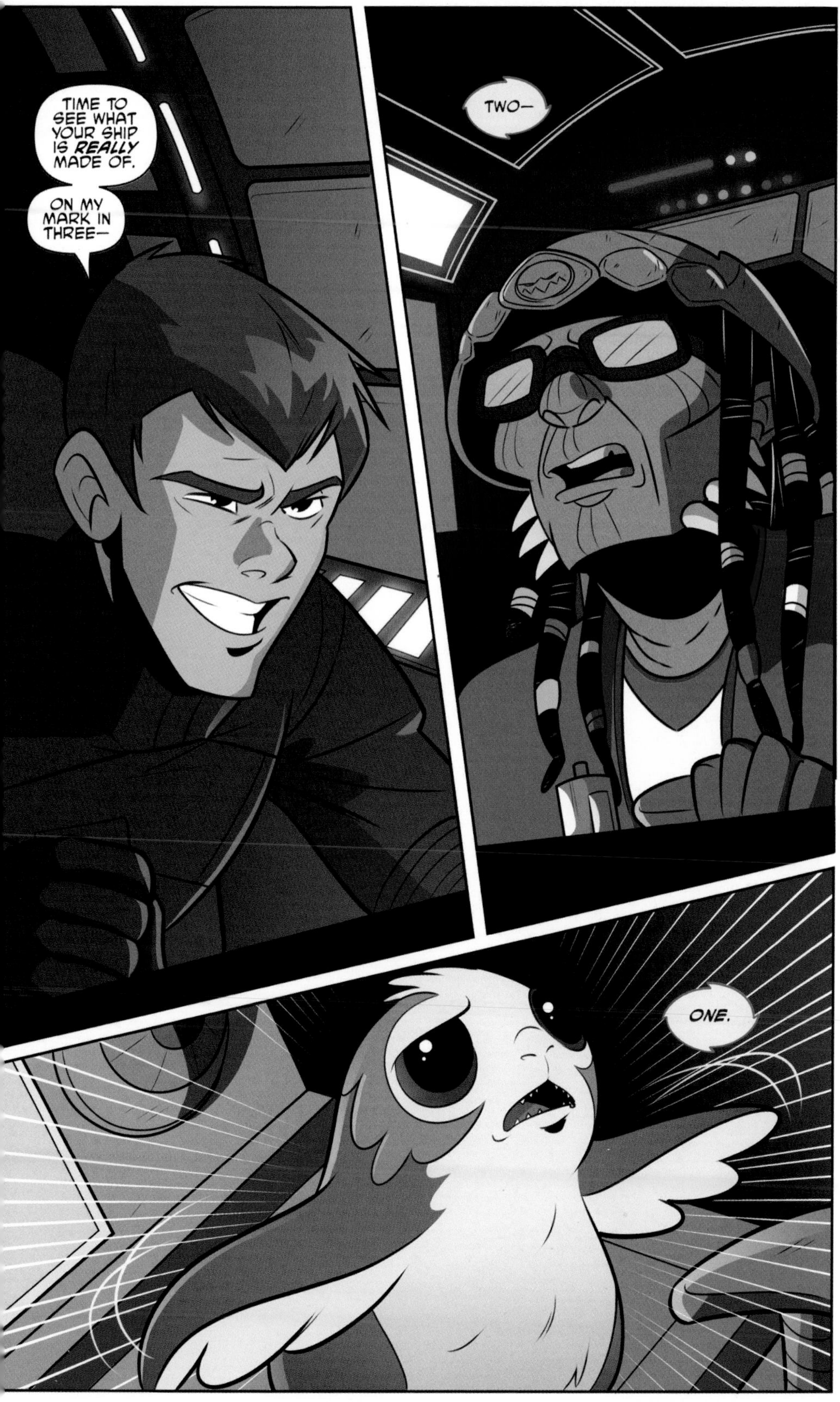
TIME TO SEE WHAT YOUR SHIP IS REALLY MADE OF.
ON MY MARK IN THREE—
TWO—
ONE.

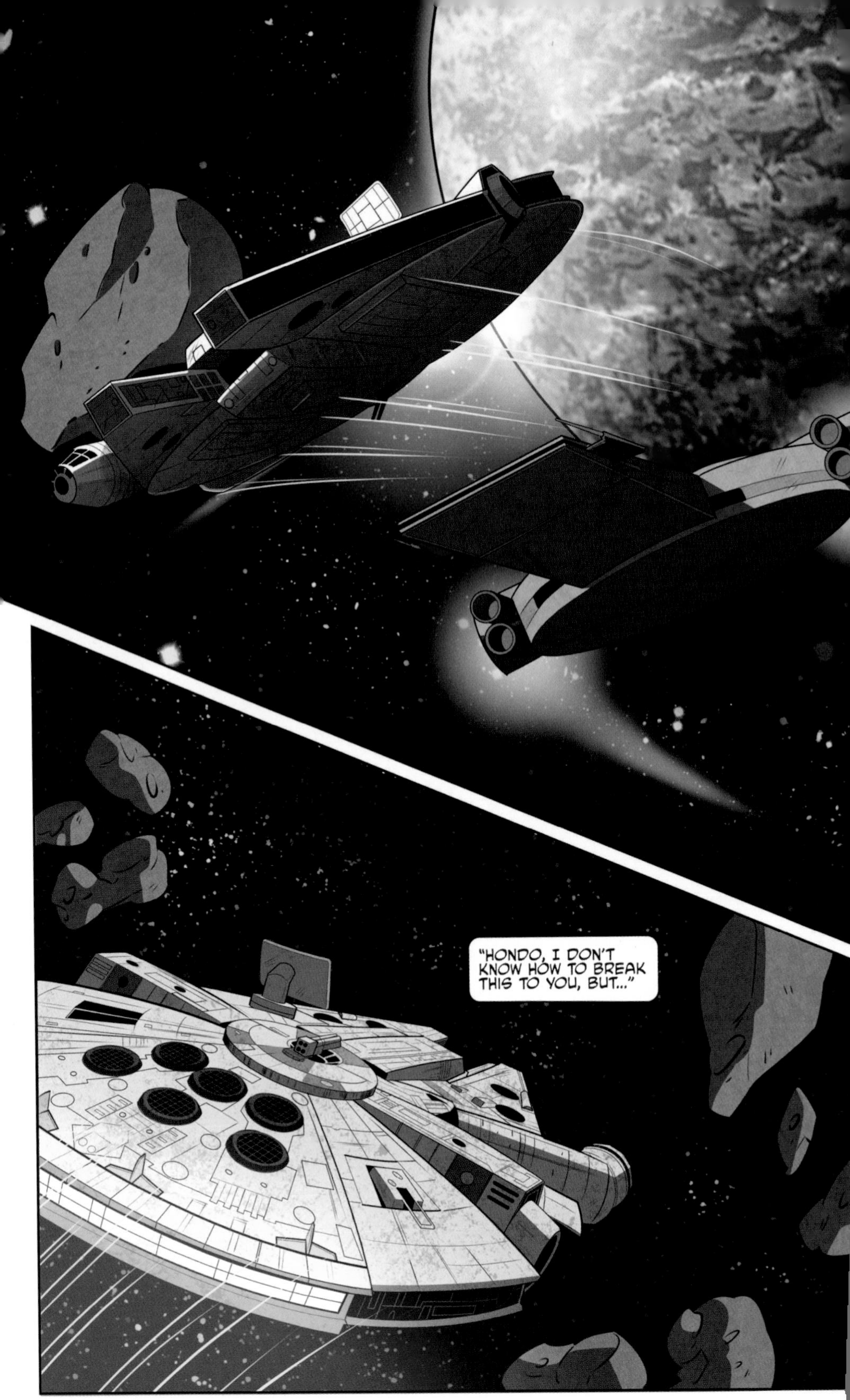
"HONDO, I DON'T KNOW HOW TO BREAK THIS TO YOU, BUT..."

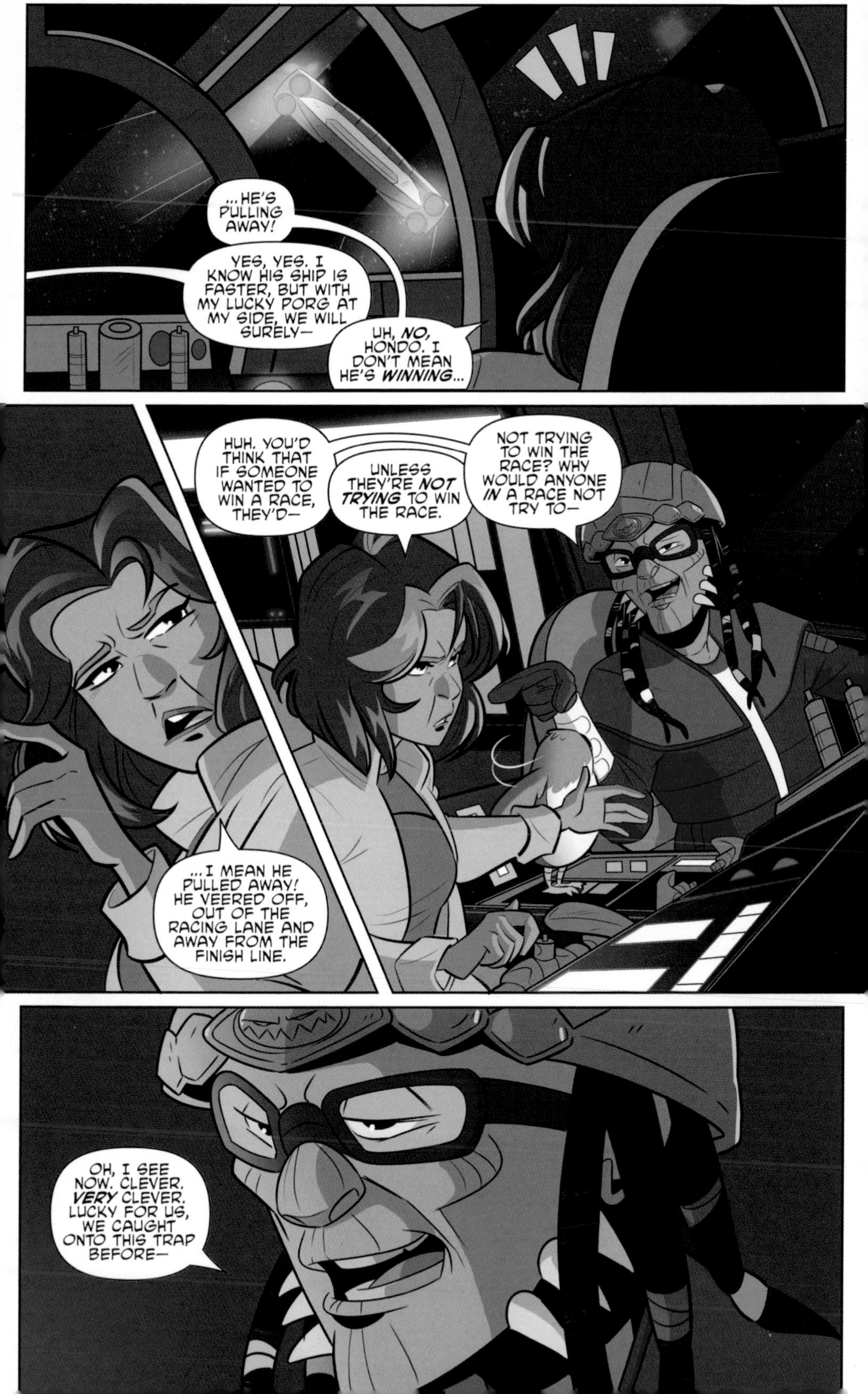
...HE'S PULLING AWAY!
YES, YES. I KNOW HIS SHIP IS FASTER, BUT WITH MY LUCKY PORG AT MY SIDE, WE WILL SURELY—
UH, NO, HONDO. I DON'T MEAN HE'S WINNING...
...I MEAN HE PULLED AWAY! HE VEERED OFF, OUT OF THE RACING LANE AND AWAY FROM THE FINISH LINE.
HUH. YOU'D THINK THAT IF SOMEONE WANTED TO WIN A RACE, THEY'D—
UNLESS THEY'RE NOT TRYING TO WIN THE RACE.
NOT TRYING TO WIN THE RACE? WHY WOULD ANYONE IN A RACE NOT TRY TO—
OH, I SEE NOW. CLEVER. VERY CLEVER. LUCKY FOR US, WE CAUGHT ONTO THIS TRAP BEFORE—

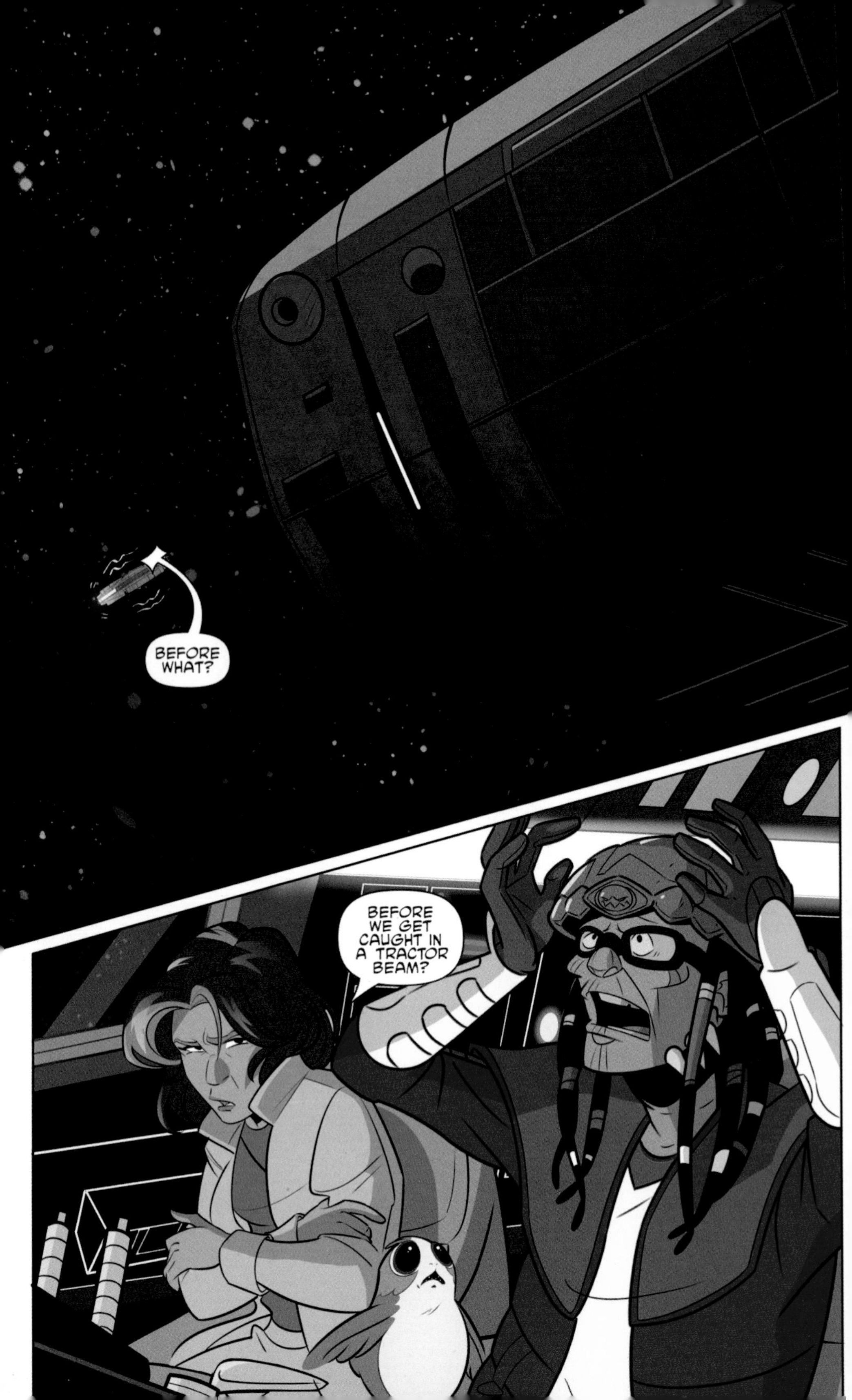
BEFORE WHAT?
BEFORE WE GET CAUGHT IN A TRACTOR BEAM?

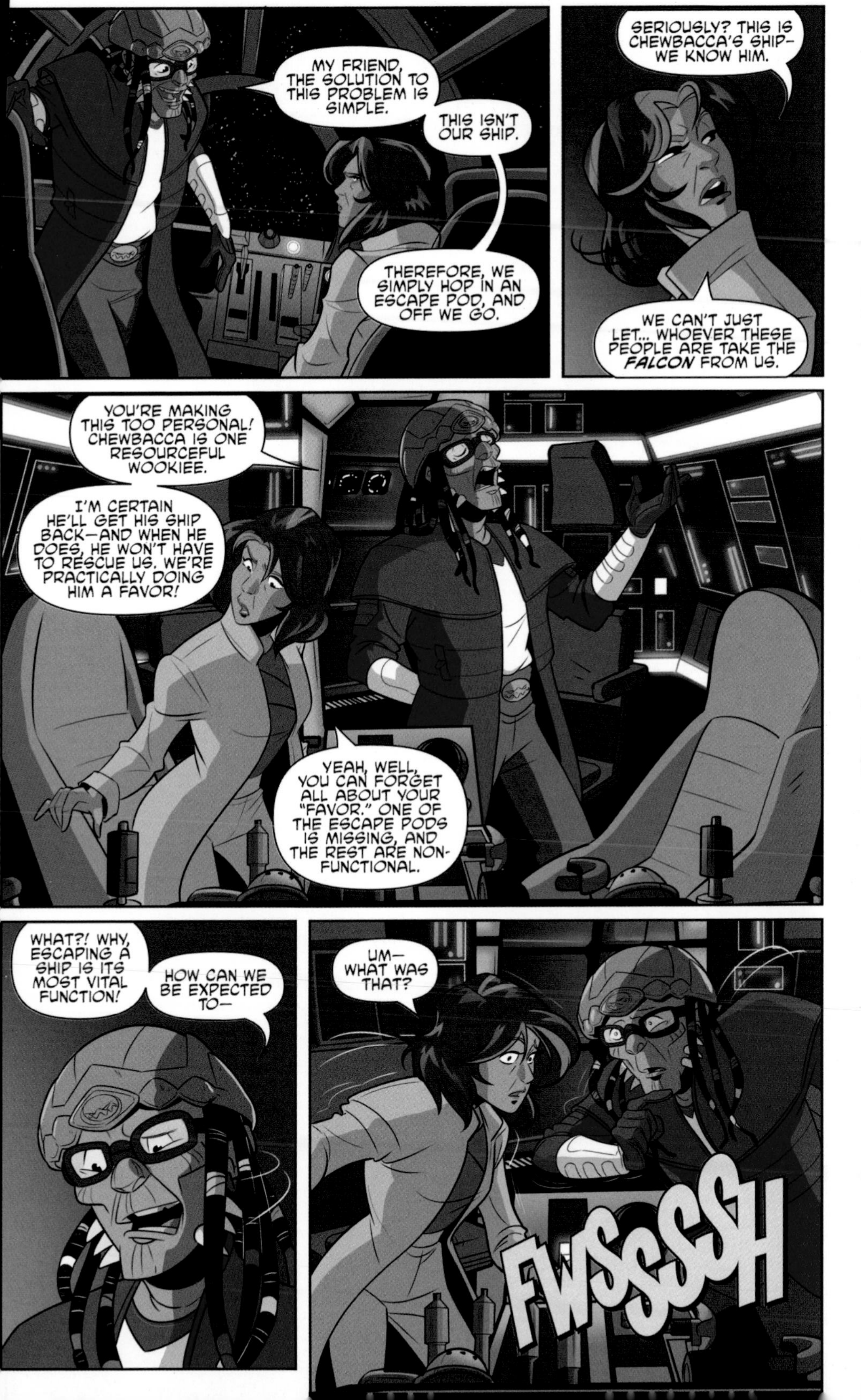
MY FRIEND, THE SOLUTION TO THIS PROBLEM IS SIMPLE.
THIS ISN'T OUR SHIP.
THEREFORE, WE SIMPLY HOP IN AN ESCAPE POD, AND OFF WE GO.
SERIOUSLY? THIS IS CHEWBACCA'S SHIP—WE KNOW HIM.
WE CAN'T JUST LET... WHOEVER THESE PEOPLE ARE TAKE THE *FALCON* FROM US.
YOU'RE MAKING THIS TOO PERSONAL! CHEWBACCA IS ONE RESOURCEFUL WOOKIEE.
I'M CERTAIN HE'LL GET HIS SHIP BACK—AND WHEN HE DOES, HE WON'T HAVE TO RESCUE US. WE'RE PRACTICALLY DOING HIM A FAVOR!
YEAH, WELL, YOU CAN FORGET ALL ABOUT YOUR "FAVOR." ONE OF THE ESCAPE PODS IS MISSING, AND THE REST ARE NON-FUNCTIONAL.
WHAT?! WHY, ESCAPING A SHIP IS ITS MOST VITAL FUNCTION!
HOW CAN WE BE EXPECTED TO—
UM—WHAT WAS THAT?
FWSSSSH

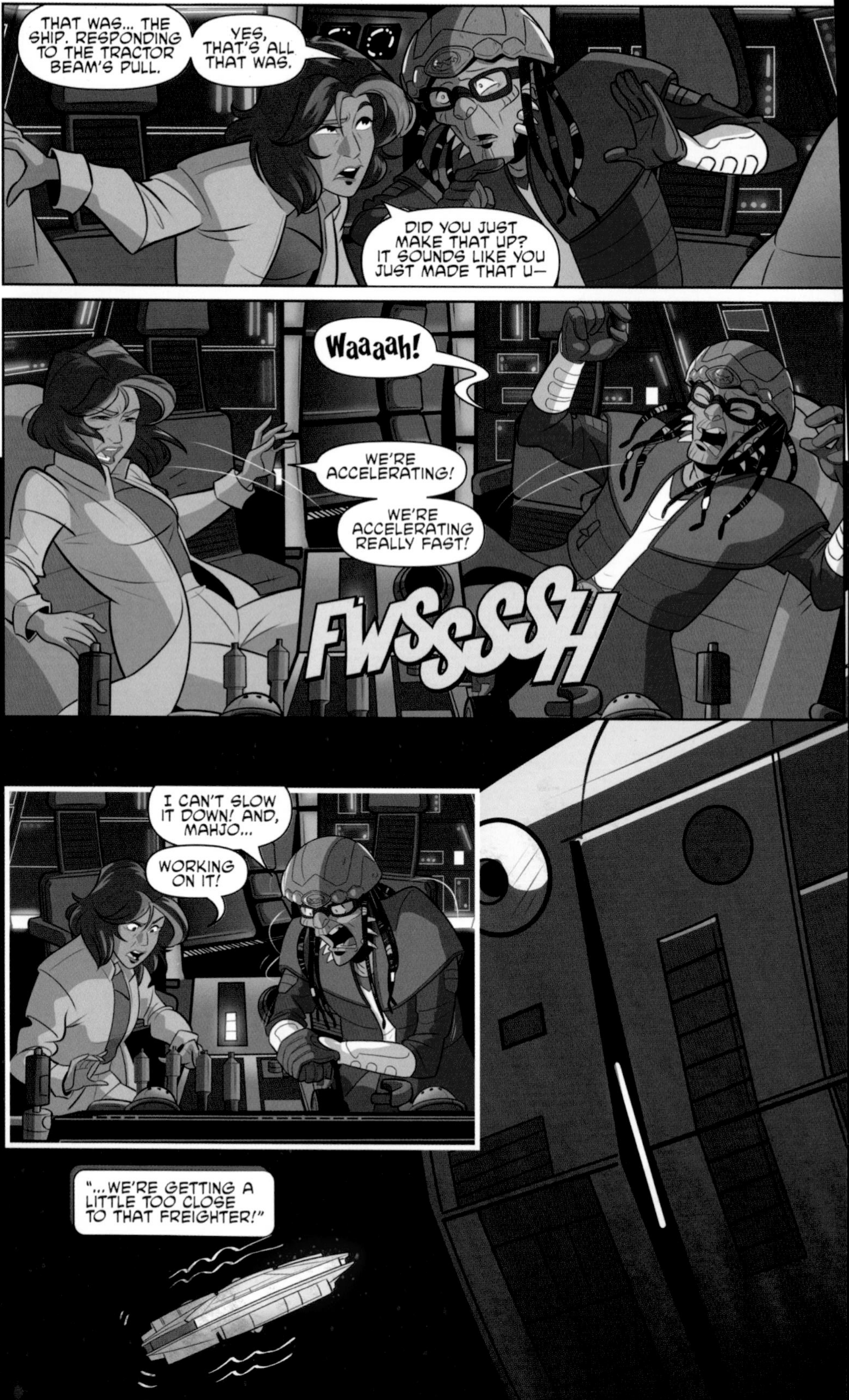
THAT WAS... THE SHIP. RESPONDING TO THE TRACTOR BEAM'S PULL.
YES, THAT'S ALL THAT WAS.
DID YOU JUST MAKE THAT UP? IT SOUNDS LIKE YOU JUST MADE THAT U—
Waaaah!
WE'RE ACCELERATING!
WE'RE ACCELERATING REALLY FAST!
FWSSSSH
I CAN'T SLOW IT DOWN! AND, MAHJO...
WORKING ON IT!
"...WE'RE GETTING A LITTLE TOO CLOSE TO THAT FREIGHTER!"

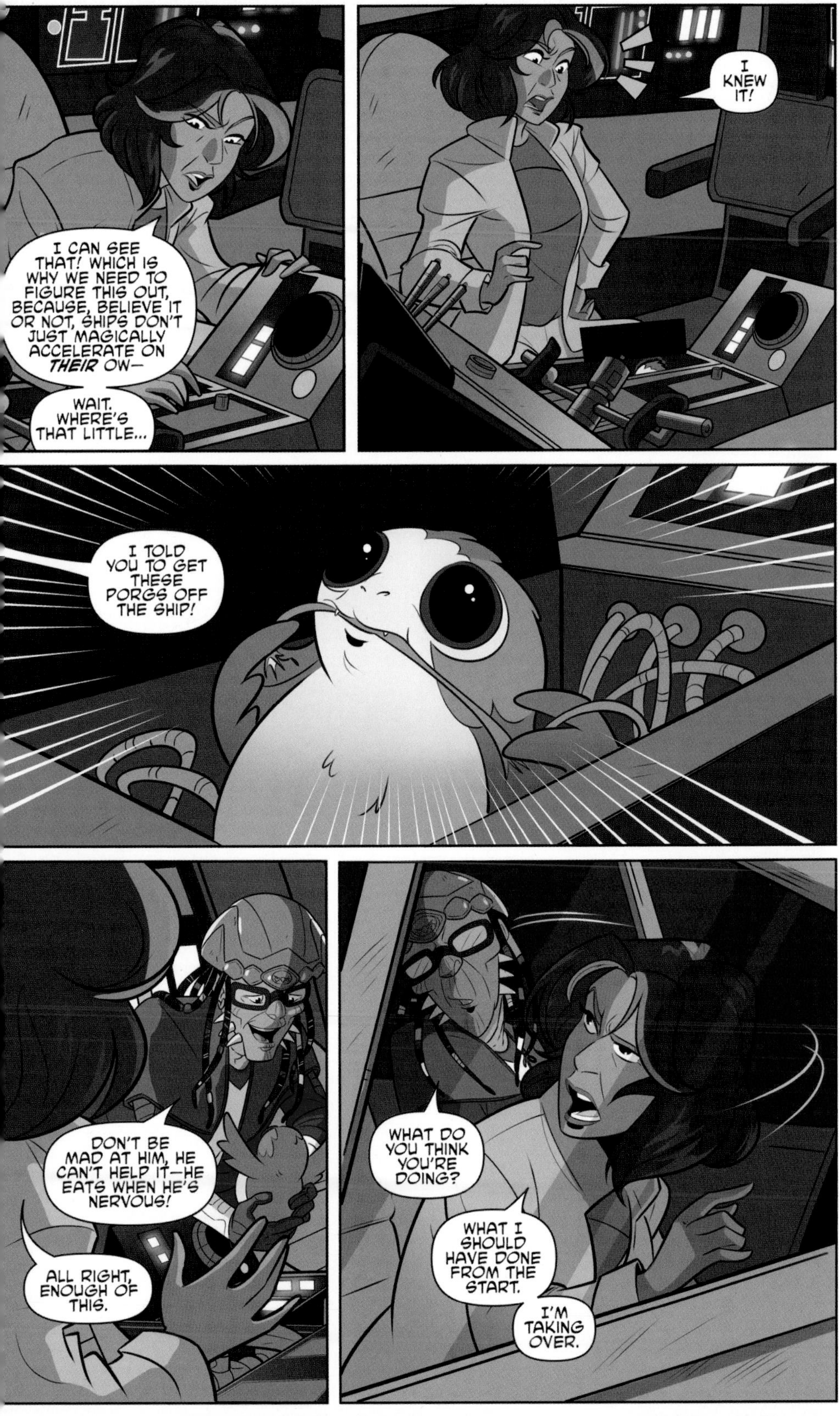
I CAN SEE THAT! WHICH IS WHY WE NEED TO FIGURE THIS OUT, BECAUSE, BELIEVE IT OR NOT, SHIPS DON'T JUST MAGICALLY ACCELERATE ON *THEIR* OW—
WAIT. WHERE'S THAT LITTLE...
I KNEW IT!
I TOLD YOU TO GET THESE PORGS OFF THE SHIP!
DON'T BE MAD AT HIM, HE CAN'T HELP IT—HE EATS WHEN HE'S NERVOUS!
ALL RIGHT, ENOUGH OF THIS.
WHAT DO YOU THINK YOU'RE DOING?
WHAT I SHOULD HAVE DONE FROM THE START.
I'M TAKING OVER.

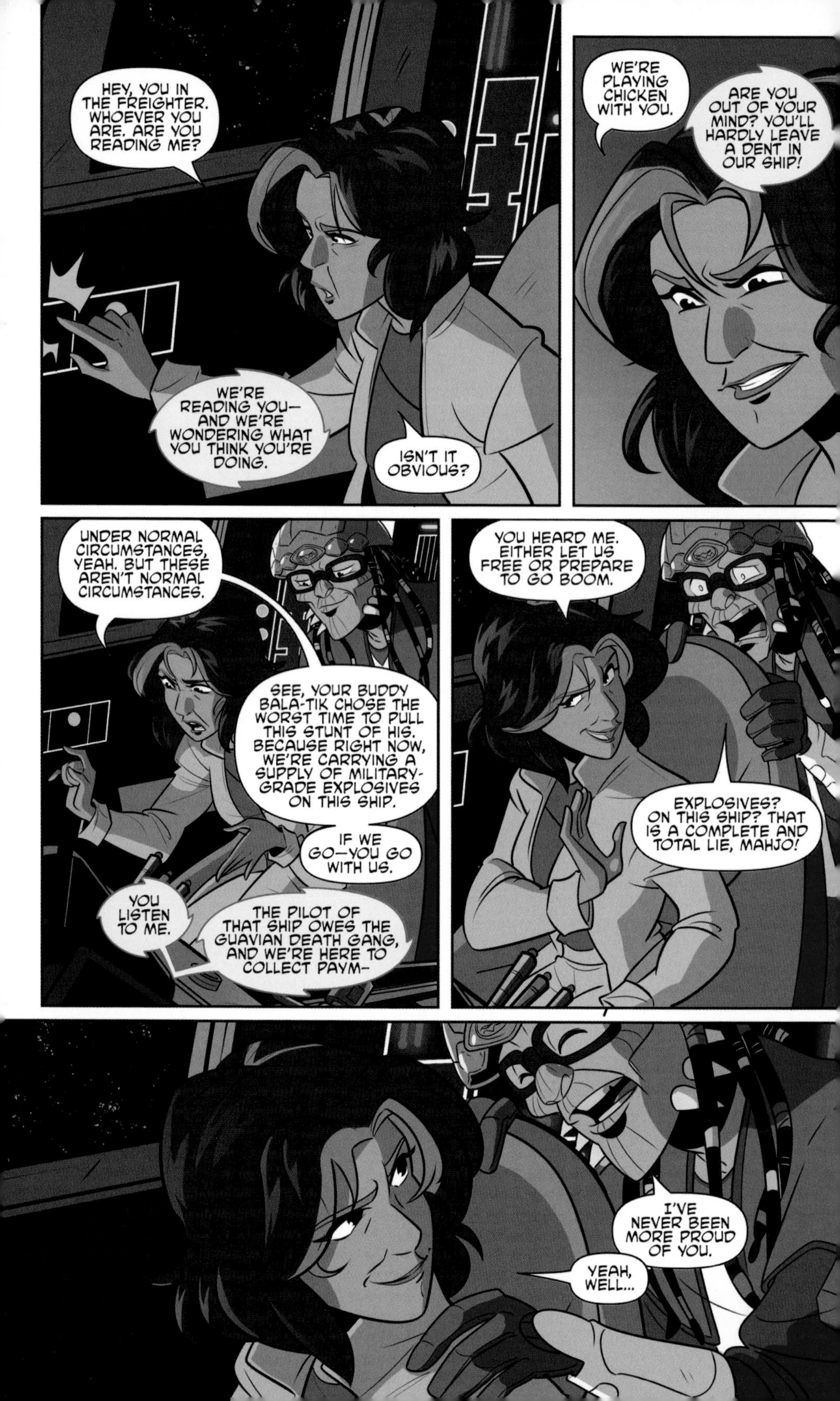

HEY, YOU IN THE FREIGHTER. WHOEVER YOU ARE. ARE YOU READING ME?
WE'RE READING YOU— AND WE'RE WONDERING WHAT YOU THINK YOU'RE DOING.
ISN'T IT OBVIOUS?
WE'RE PLAYING CHICKEN WITH YOU.
ARE YOU OUT OF YOUR MIND? YOU'LL HARDLY LEAVE A DENT IN OUR SHIP!
UNDER NORMAL CIRCUMSTANCES, YEAH. BUT THESE AREN'T NORMAL CIRCUMSTANCES.
SEE, YOUR BUDDY BALA-TIK CHOSE THE WORST TIME TO PULL THIS STUNT OF HIS. BECAUSE RIGHT NOW, WE'RE CARRYING A SUPPLY OF MILITARY-GRADE EXPLOSIVES ON THIS SHIP.
IF WE GO—YOU GO WITH US.
YOU LISTEN TO ME.
THE PILOT OF THAT SHIP OWES THE GUAVIAN DEATH GANG, AND WE'RE HERE TO COLLECT PAYM-
YOU HEARD ME. EITHER LET US FREE OR PREPARE TO GO BOOM.
EXPLOSIVES? ON THIS SHIP? THAT IS A COMPLETE AND TOTAL LIE, MAHJO!
I'VE NEVER BEEN MORE PROUD OF YOU.
YEAH, WELL...

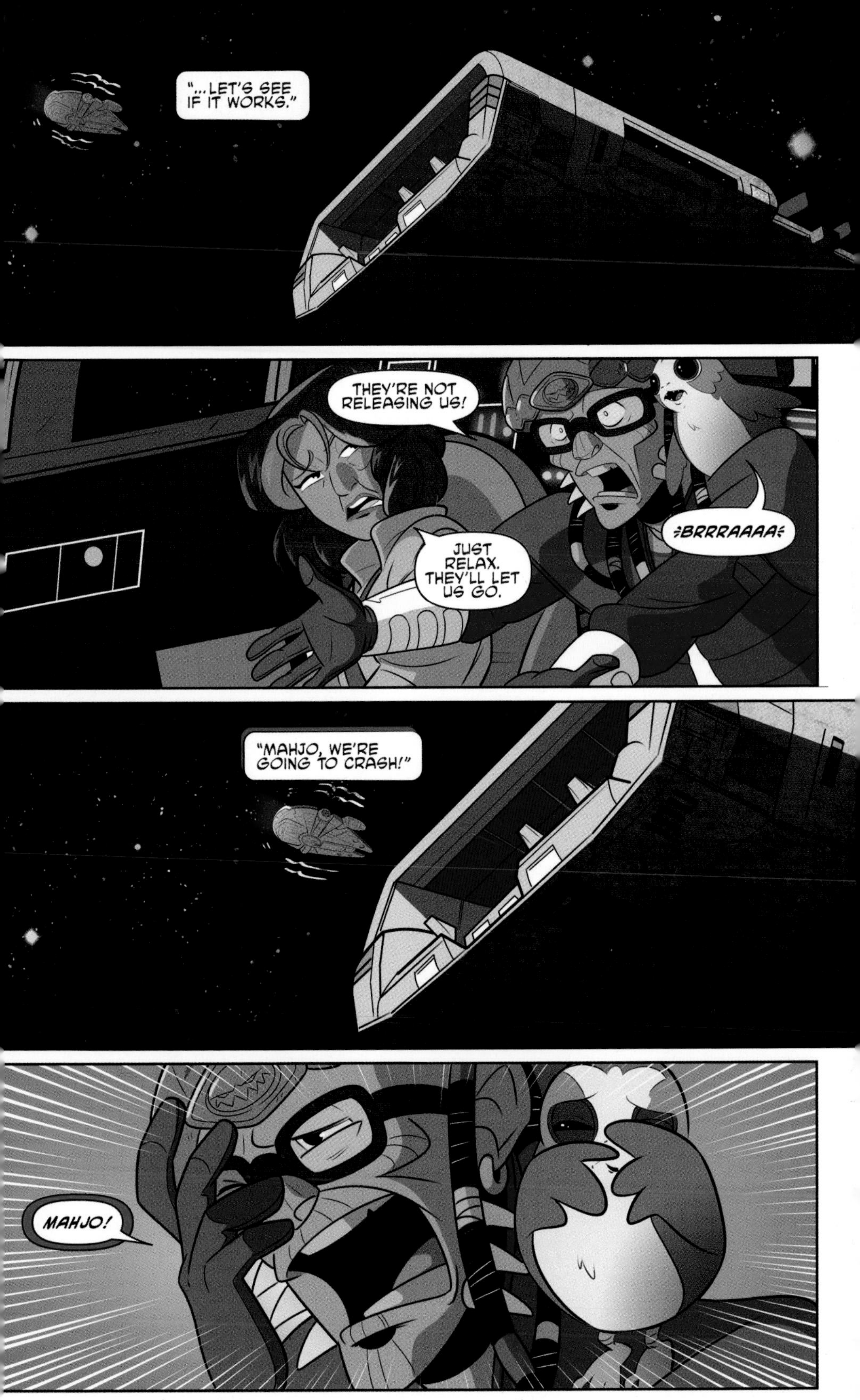
"...LET'S SEE IF IT WORKS."
THEY'RE NOT RELEASING US!
JUST RELAX. THEY'LL LET US GO.
BRRRAAAA
"MAHJO, WE'RE GOING TO CRASH!"
MAHJO!

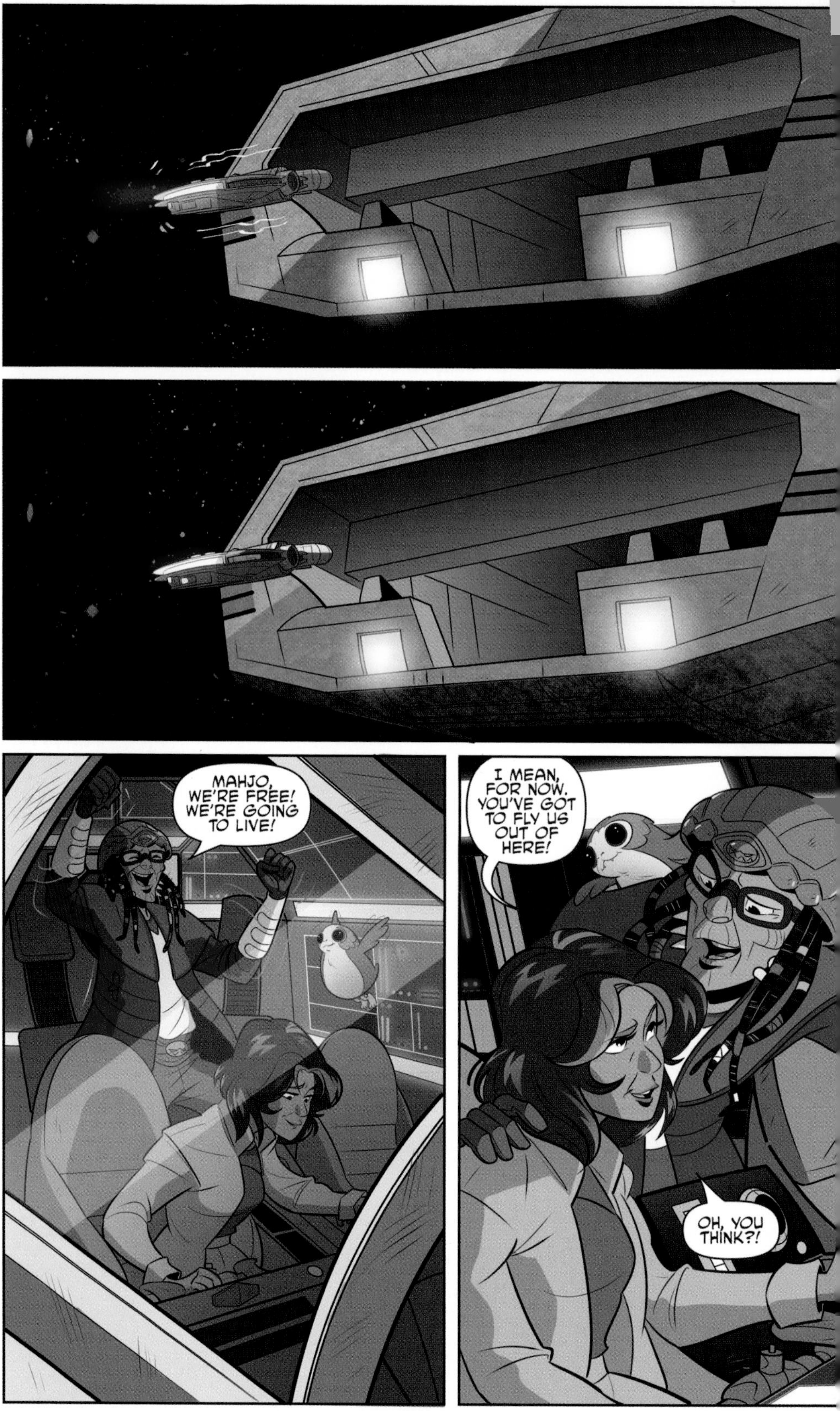

MAHJO, WE'RE FREE! WE'RE GOING TO LIVE!
I MEAN, FOR NOW. YOU'VE GOT TO FLY US OUT OF HERE!
OH, YOU THINK?!

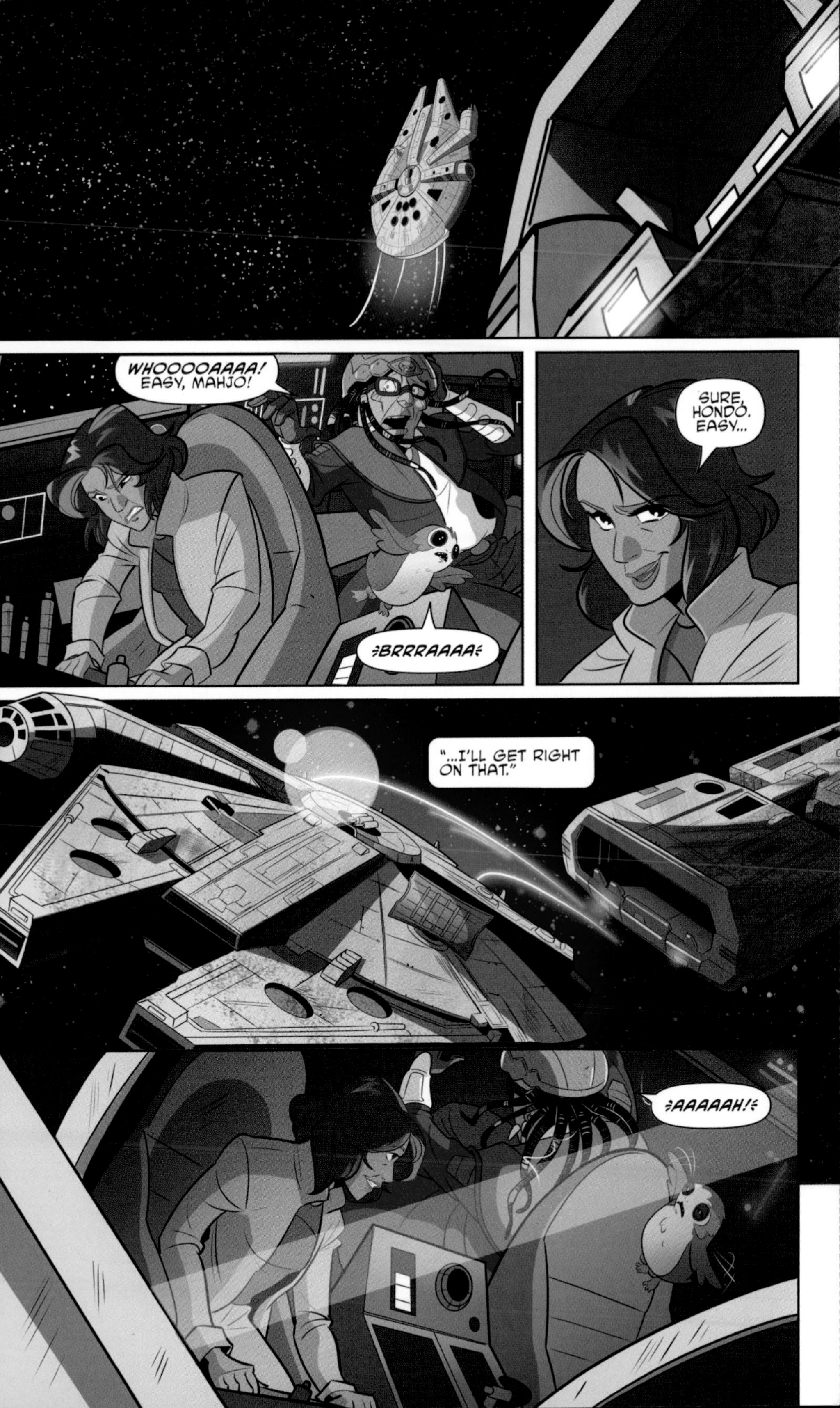
WHOOOOAAAA! EASY, MAHJO!
BRRRAAAA
SURE, HONDO. EASY...
"...I'LL GET RIGHT ON THAT."
AAAAAH!

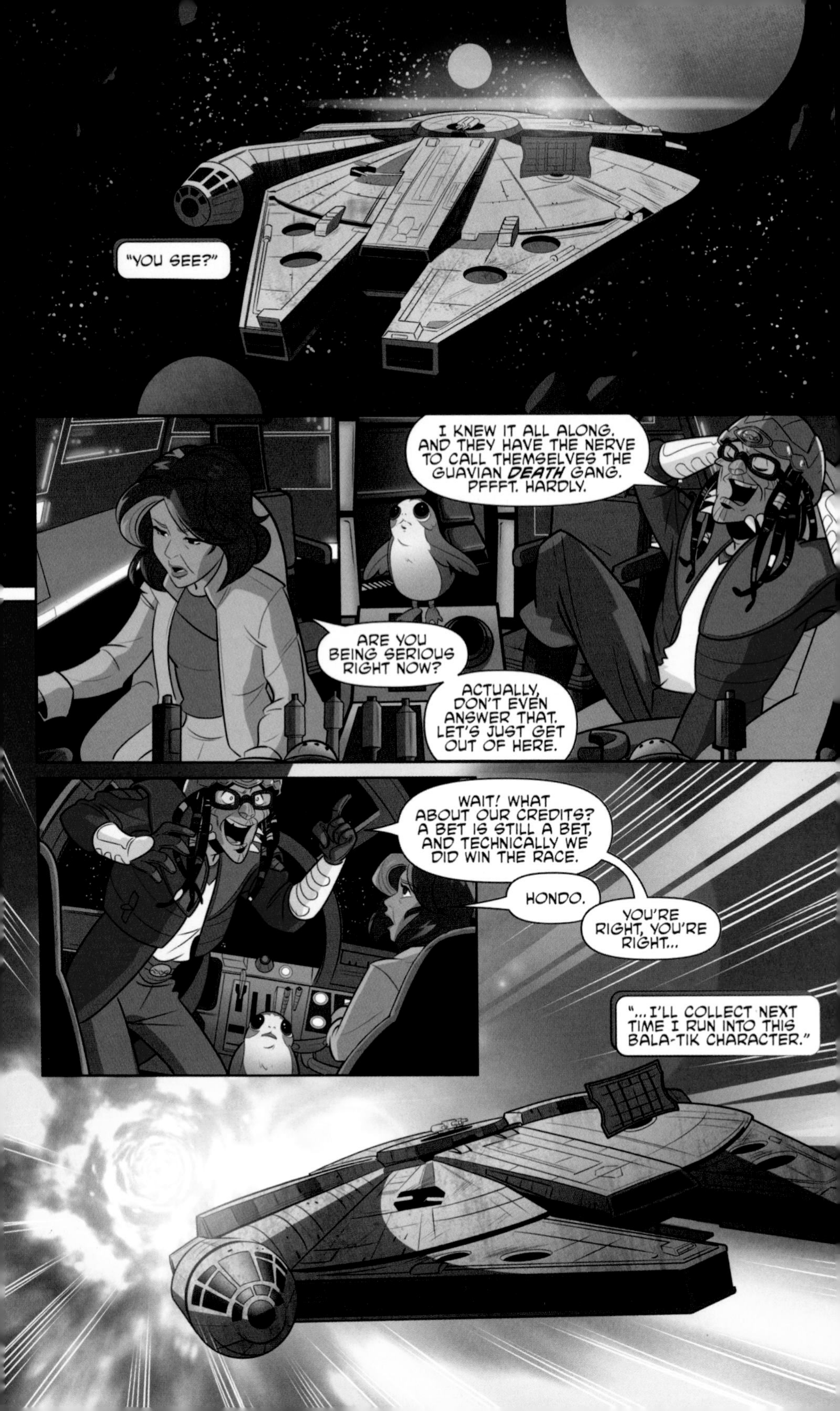
"YOU SEE?"
I KNEW IT ALL ALONG. AND THEY HAVE THE NERVE TO CALL THEMSELVES THE GUAVIAN *DEATH* GANG. PFFFT. HARDLY.
ARE YOU BEING SERIOUS RIGHT NOW?
ACTUALLY, DON'T EVEN ANSWER THAT. LET'S JUST GET OUT OF HERE.
WAIT! WHAT ABOUT OUR CREDITS? A BET IS STILL A BET, AND TECHNICALLY WE DID WIN THE RACE.
HONDO.
YOU'RE RIGHT, YOU'RE RIGHT...
"...I'LL COLLECT NEXT TIME I RUN INTO THIS BALA-TIK CHARACTER."

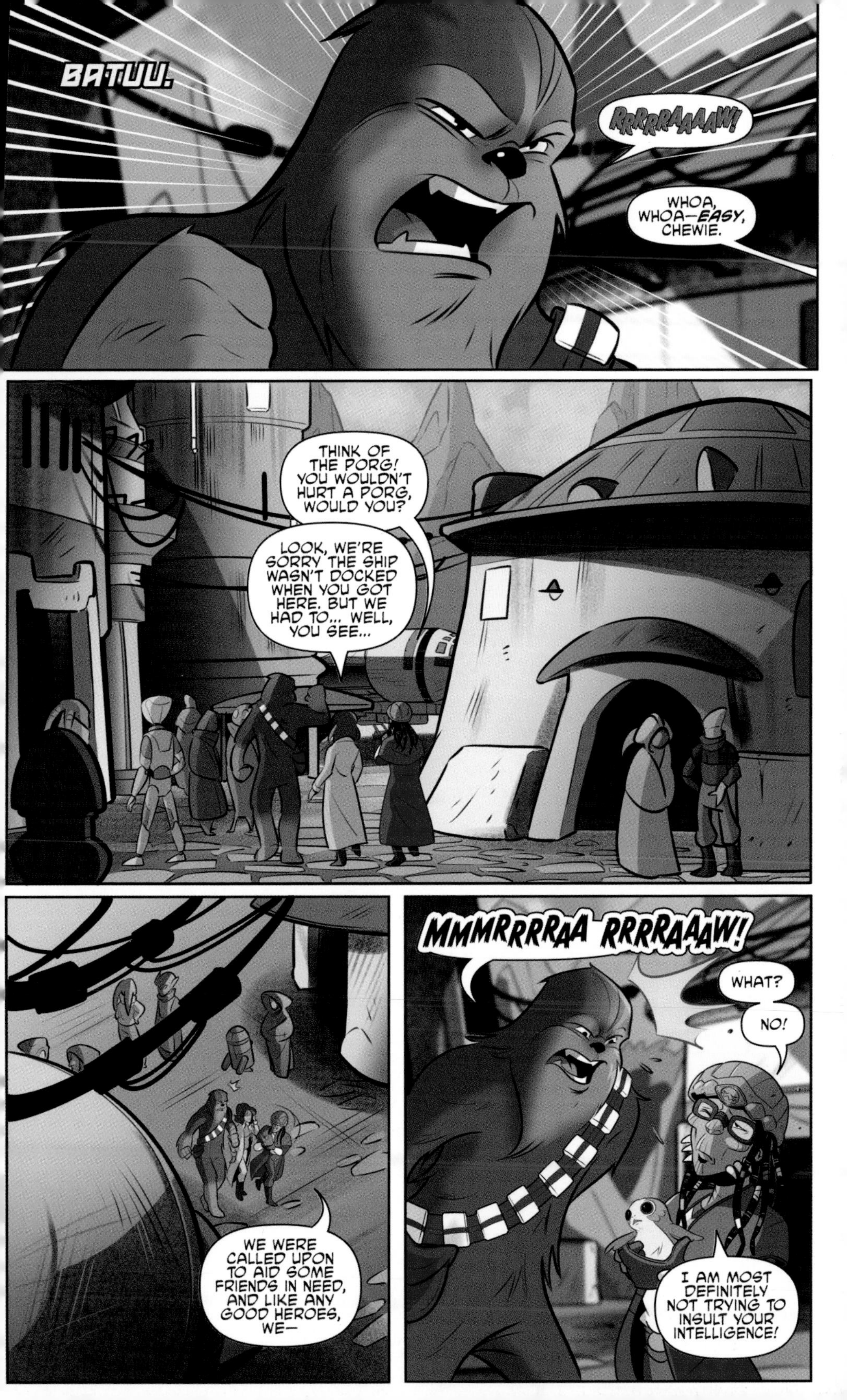
BATUU.
RRRRRAAAAW!
WHOA, WHOA—EASY, CHEWIE.
THINK OF THE PORG! YOU WOULDN'T HURT A PORG, WOULD YOU?
LOOK, WE'RE SORRY THE SHIP WASN'T DOCKED WHEN YOU GOT HERE. BUT WE HAD TO... WELL, YOU SEE...
WE WERE CALLED UPON TO AID SOME FRIENDS IN NEED, AND LIKE ANY GOOD HEROES, WE—
MMMRRRRAA RRRRAAAW!
WHAT?
NO!
I AM MOST DEFINITELY NOT TRYING TO INSULT YOUR INTELLIGENCE!

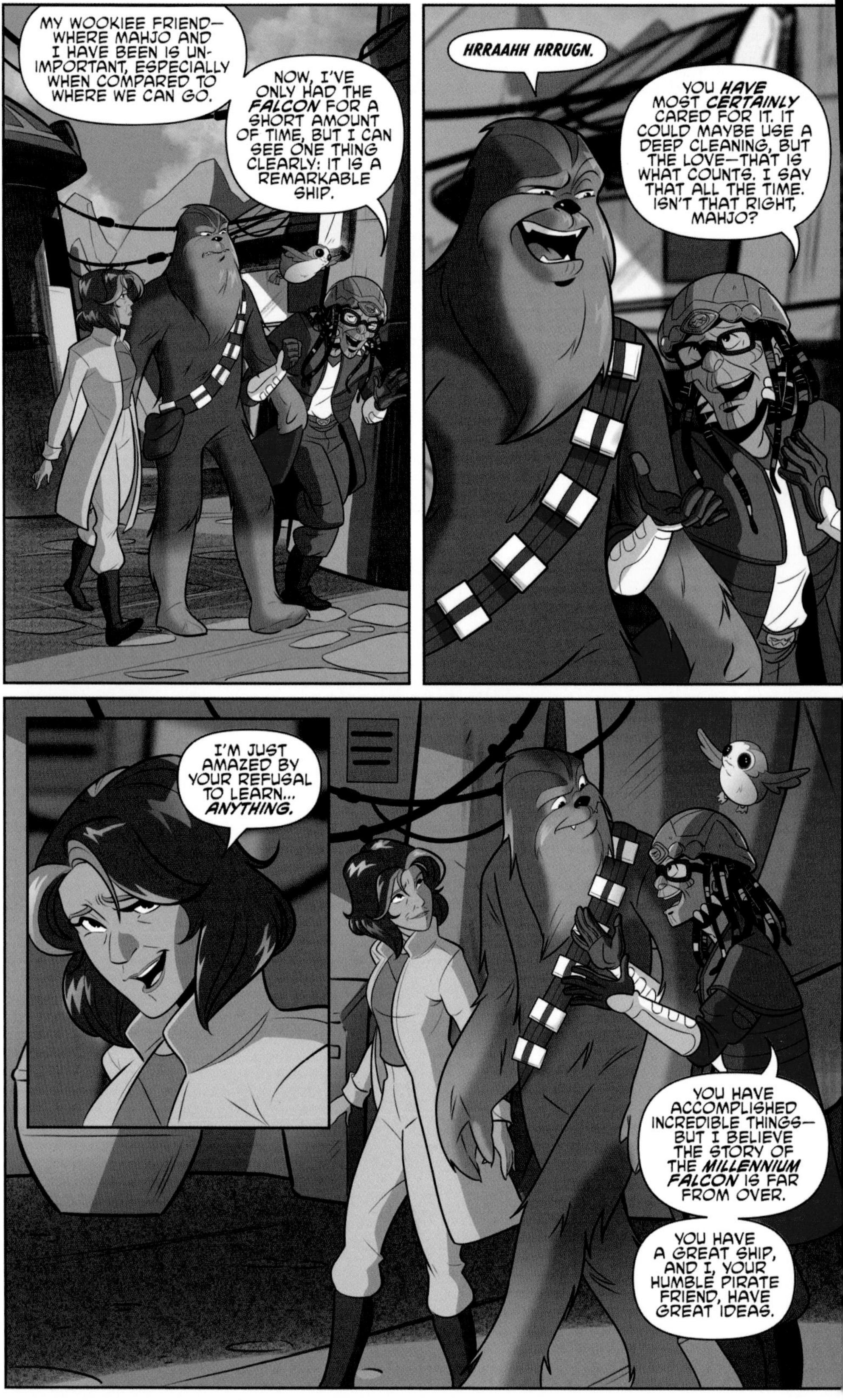
MY WOOKIEE FRIEND—WHERE MAHJO AND I HAVE BEEN IS UN-IMPORTANT, ESPECIALLY WHEN COMPARED TO WHERE WE CAN GO.
NOW, I'VE ONLY HAD THE *FALCON* FOR A SHORT AMOUNT OF TIME, BUT I CAN SEE ONE THING CLEARLY: IT IS A REMARKABLE SHIP.
HRRAAHH HRRUGN.
YOU *HAVE* MOST *CERTAINLY* CARED FOR IT. IT COULD MAYBE USE A DEEP CLEANING, BUT THE LOVE—THAT IS WHAT COUNTS. I SAY THAT ALL THE TIME. ISN'T THAT RIGHT, MAHJO?
I'M JUST AMAZED BY YOUR REFUSAL TO LEARN... *ANYTHING.*
YOU HAVE ACCOMPLISHED INCREDIBLE THINGS—BUT I BELIEVE THE STORY OF THE *MILLENNIUM FALCON* IS FAR FROM OVER.
YOU HAVE A GREAT SHIP, AND I, YOUR HUMBLE PIRATE FRIEND, HAVE GREAT IDEAS.

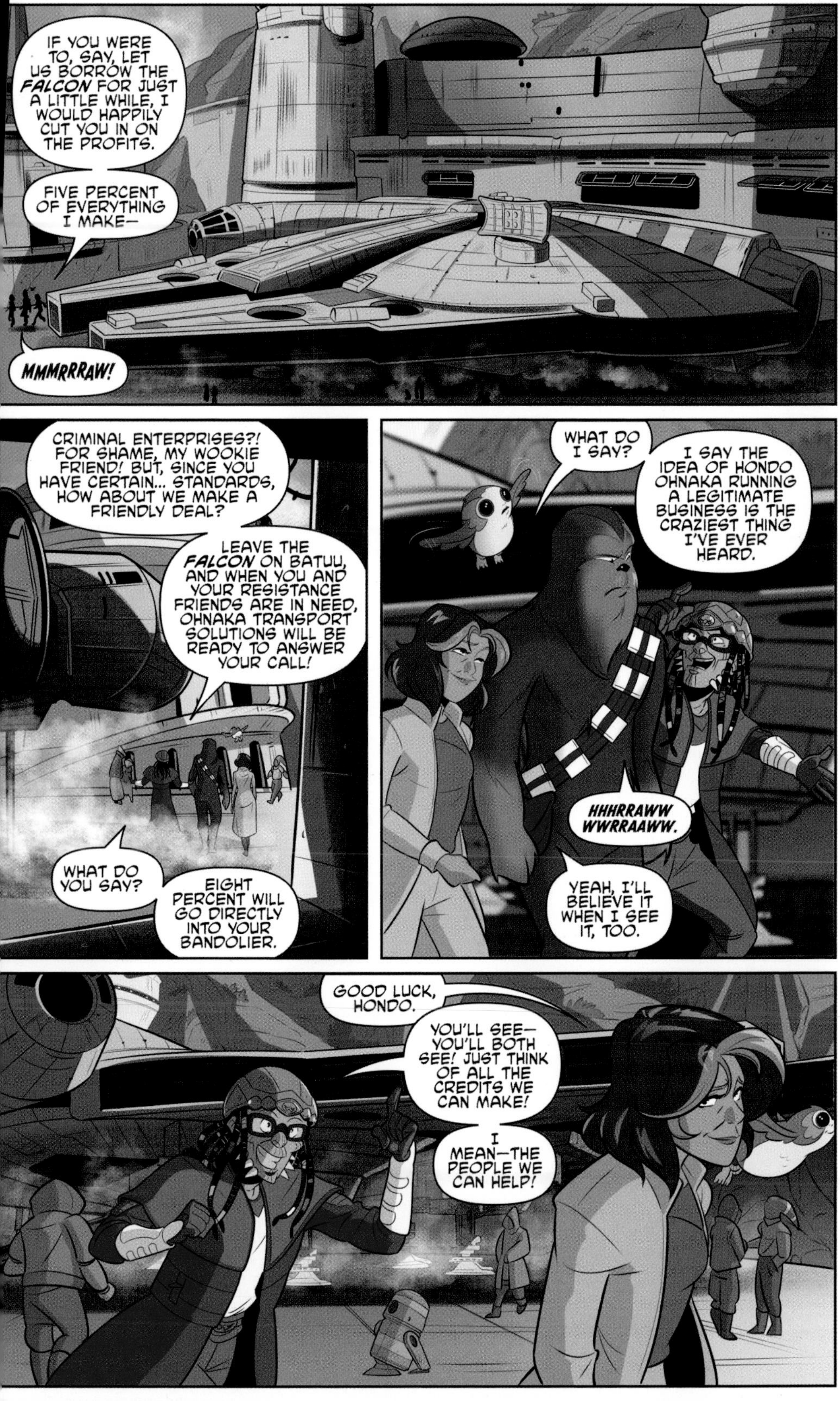
IF YOU WERE TO, SAY, LET US BORROW THE *FALCON* FOR JUST A LITTLE WHILE, I WOULD HAPPILY CUT YOU IN ON THE PROFITS.
FIVE PERCENT OF EVERYTHING I MAKE—
MMMRRRAW!
CRIMINAL ENTERPRISES?! FOR SHAME, MY WOOKIE FRIEND! BUT, SINCE YOU HAVE CERTAIN... STANDARDS, HOW ABOUT WE MAKE A FRIENDLY DEAL?
LEAVE THE *FALCON* ON BATUU, AND WHEN YOU AND YOUR RESISTANCE FRIENDS ARE IN NEED, OHNAKA TRANSPORT SOLUTIONS WILL BE READY TO ANSWER YOUR CALL!
WHAT DO YOU SAY?
EIGHT PERCENT WILL GO DIRECTLY INTO YOUR BANDOLIER.
WHAT DO I SAY?
I SAY THE IDEA OF HONDO OHNAKA RUNNING A LEGITIMATE BUSINESS IS THE CRAZIEST THING I'VE EVER HEARD.
HHHRRAWW WWRRAAWW.
YEAH, I'LL BELIEVE IT WHEN I SEE IT, TOO.
GOOD LUCK, HONDO.
YOU'LL SEE— YOU'LL BOTH SEE! JUST THINK OF ALL THE CREDITS WE CAN MAKE!
I MEAN—THE PEOPLE WE CAN HELP!

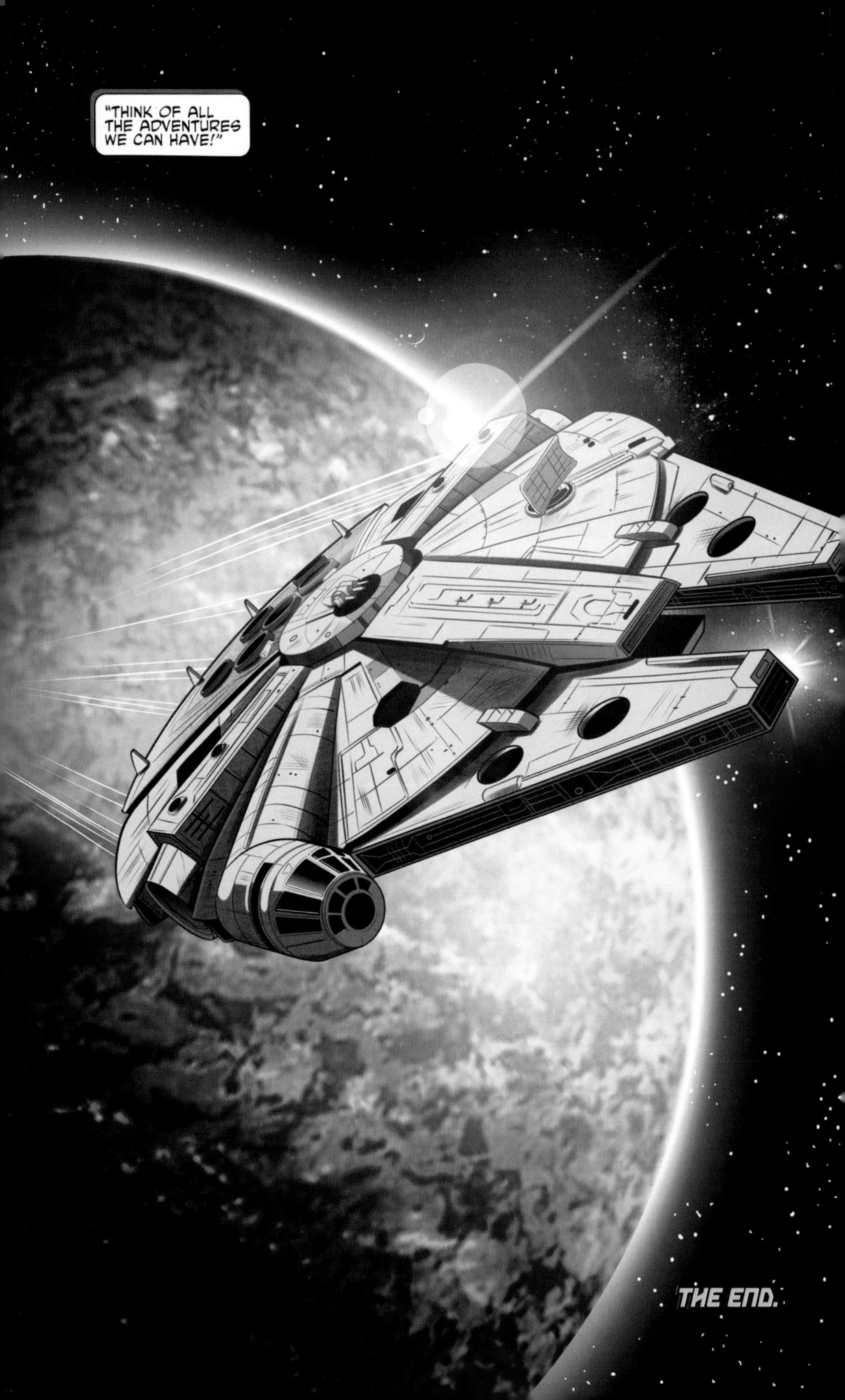
"THINK OF ALL THE ADVENTURES WE CAN HAVE!"
THE END.

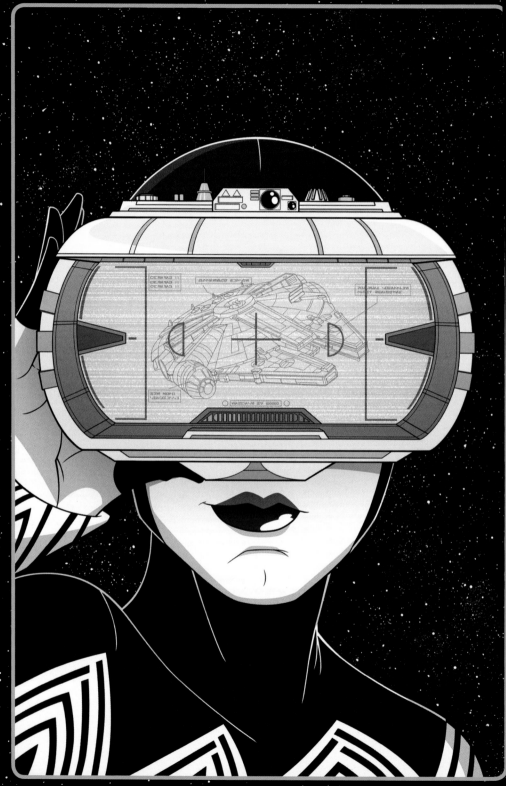

Art by Philip Murphy

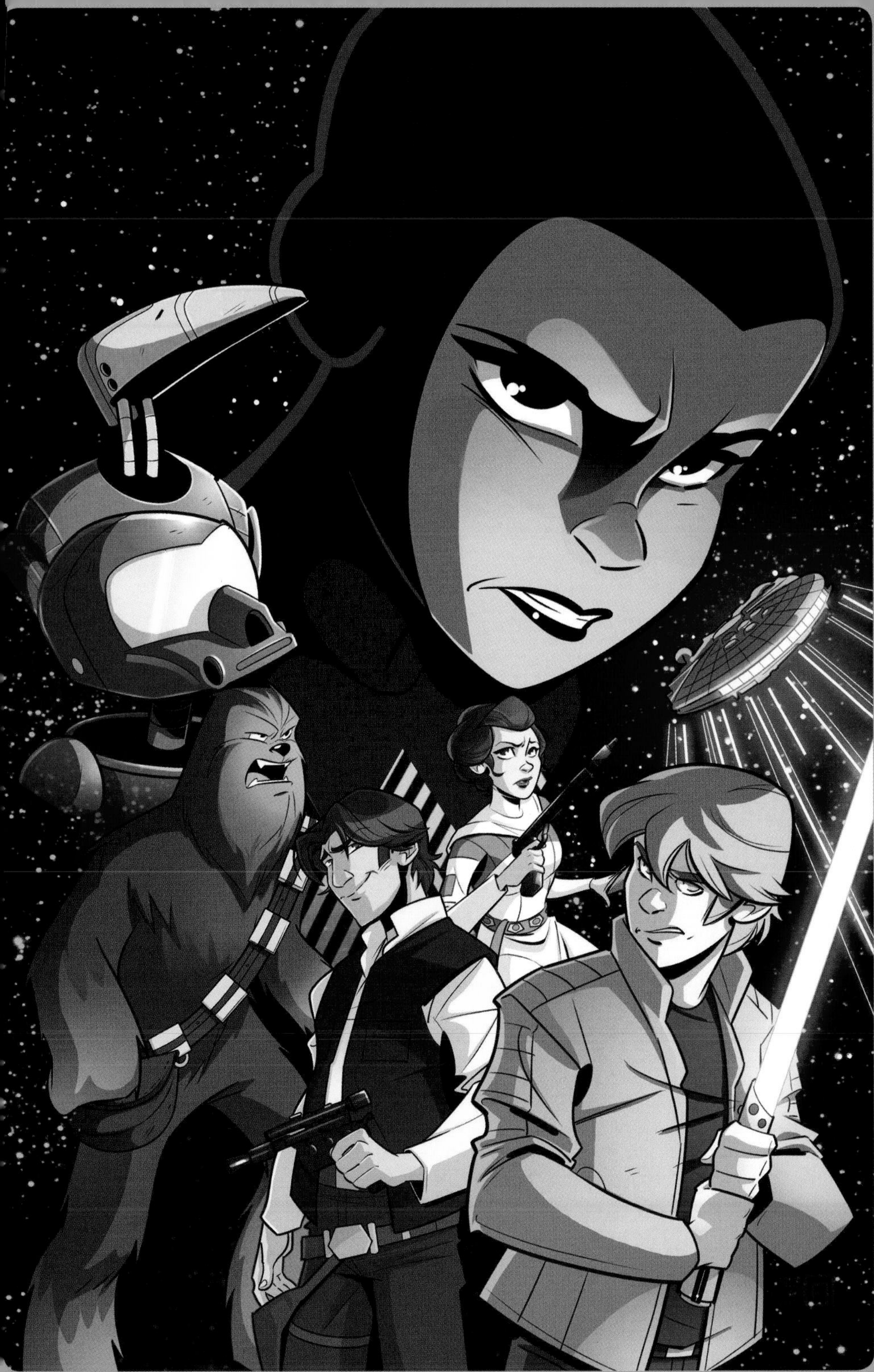

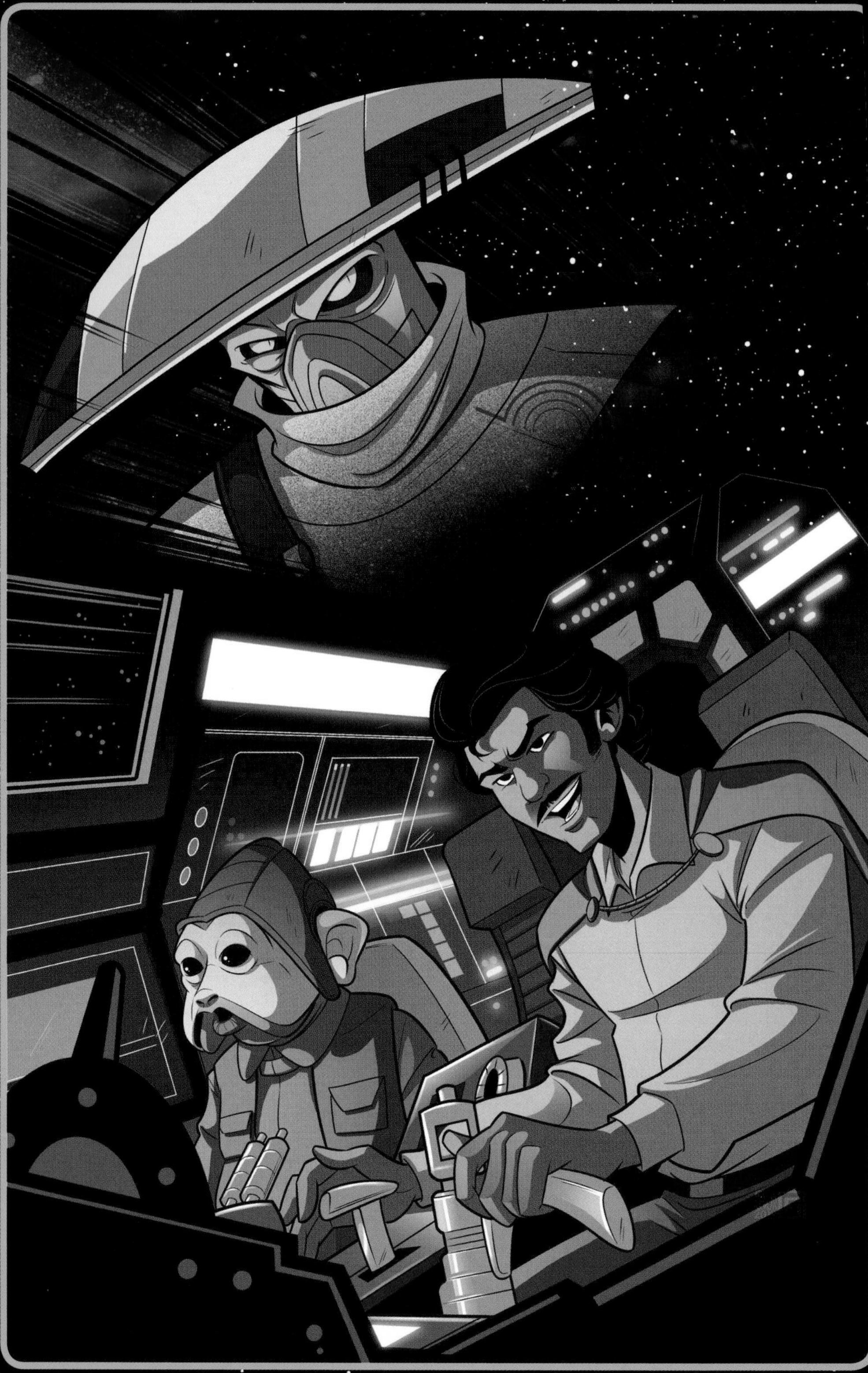

Art by Arianna Florean

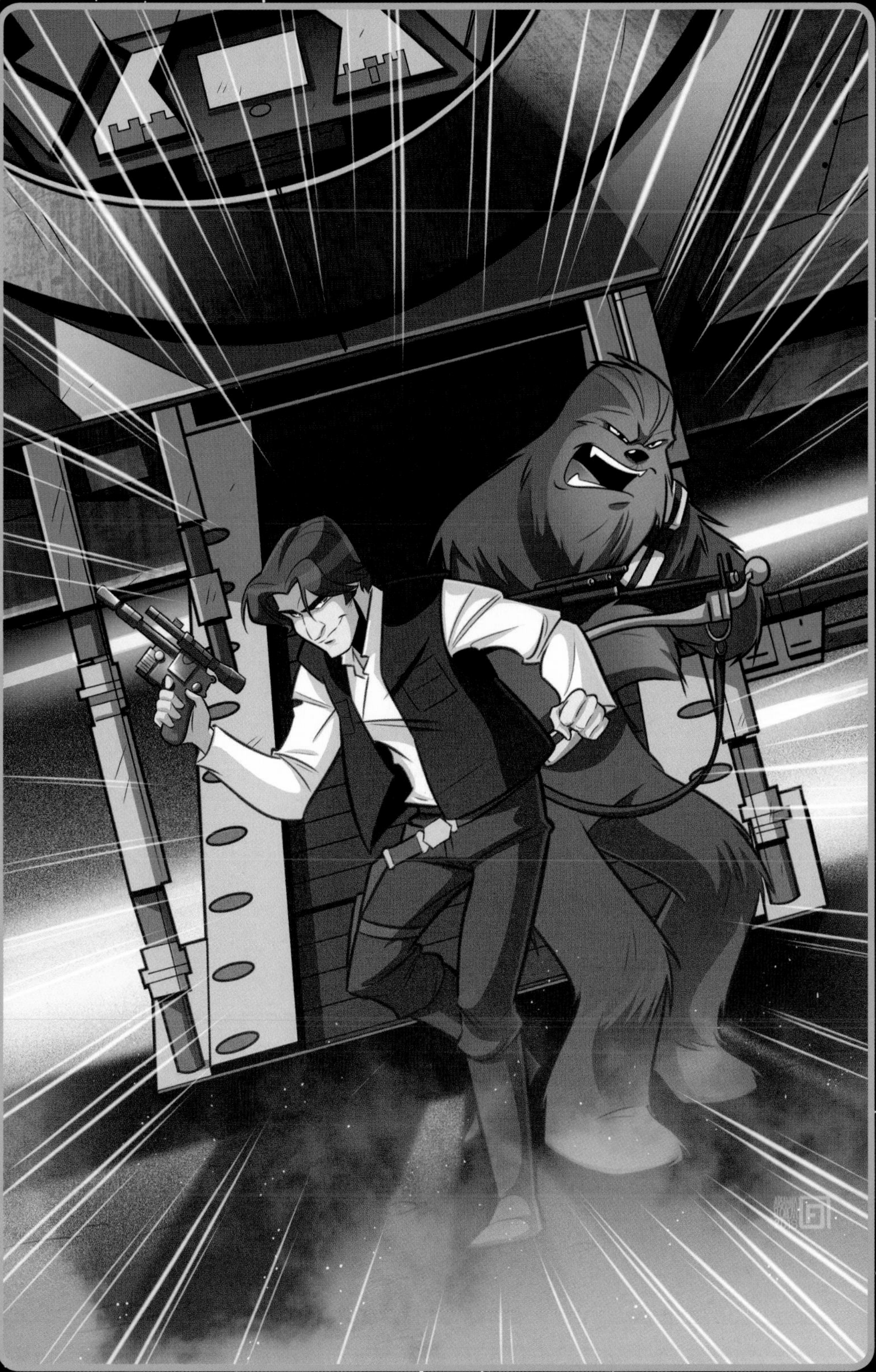

Art by Arianna Florean

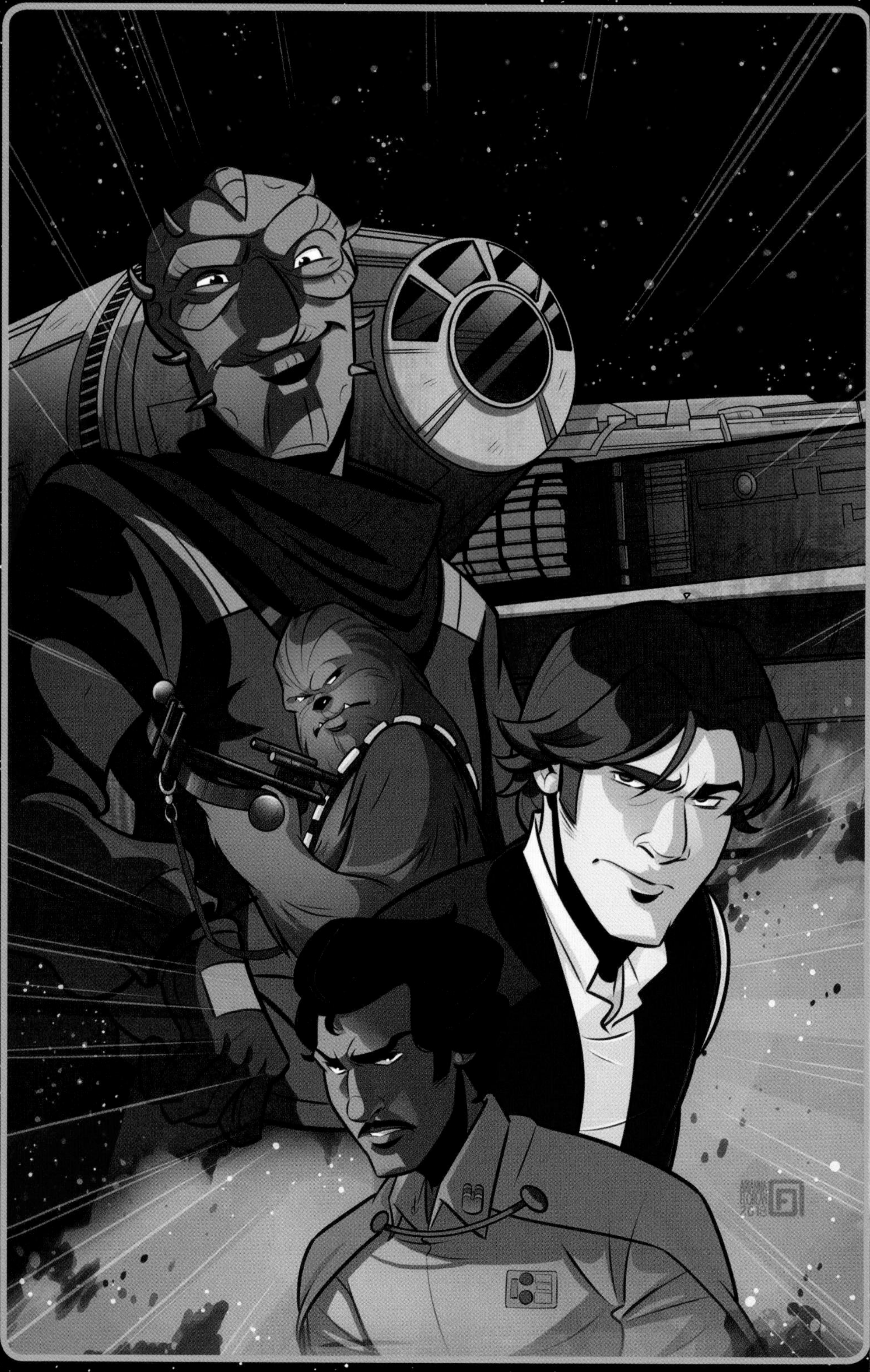

Art by Arianna Florean

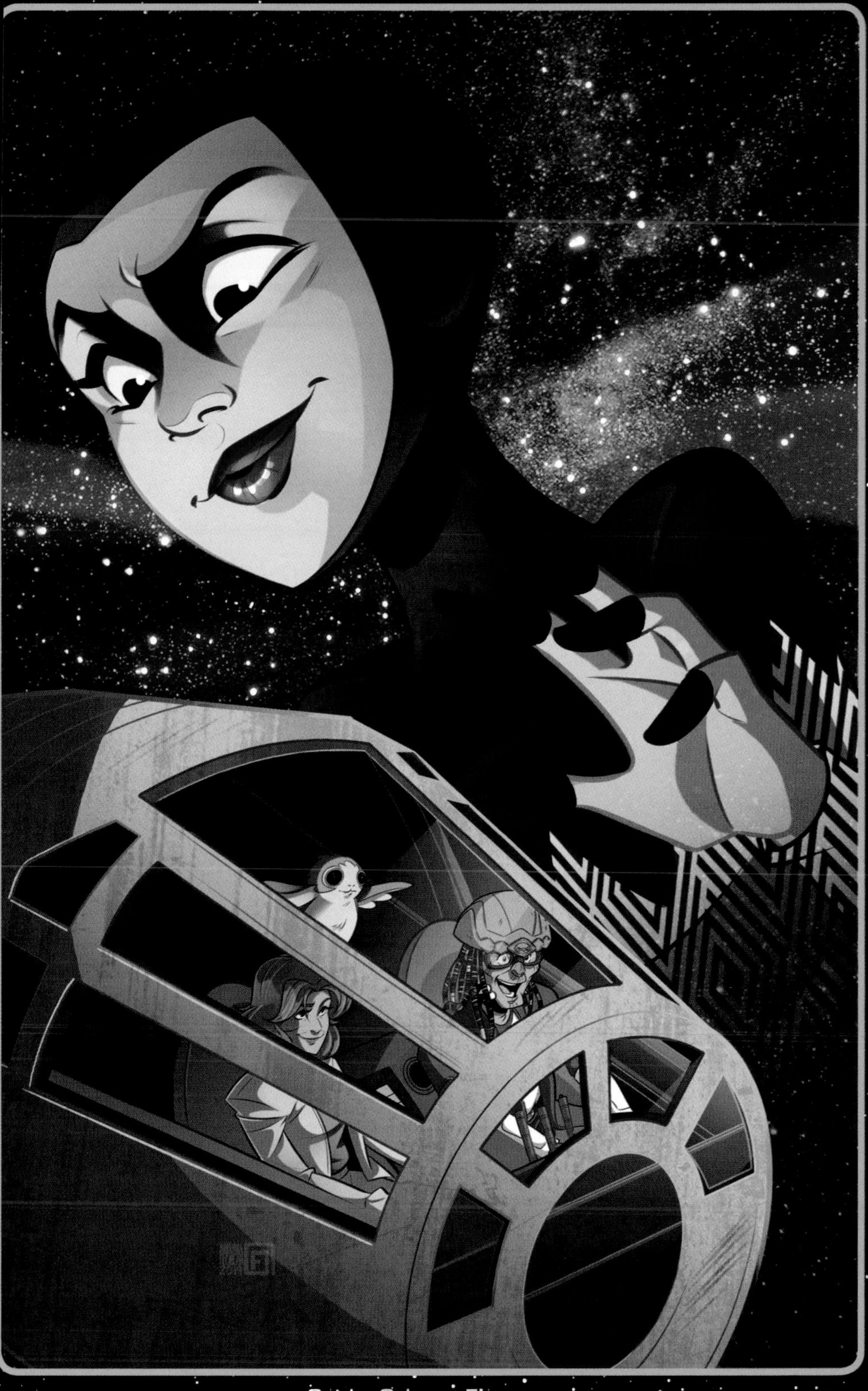

Art by Arianna Florean

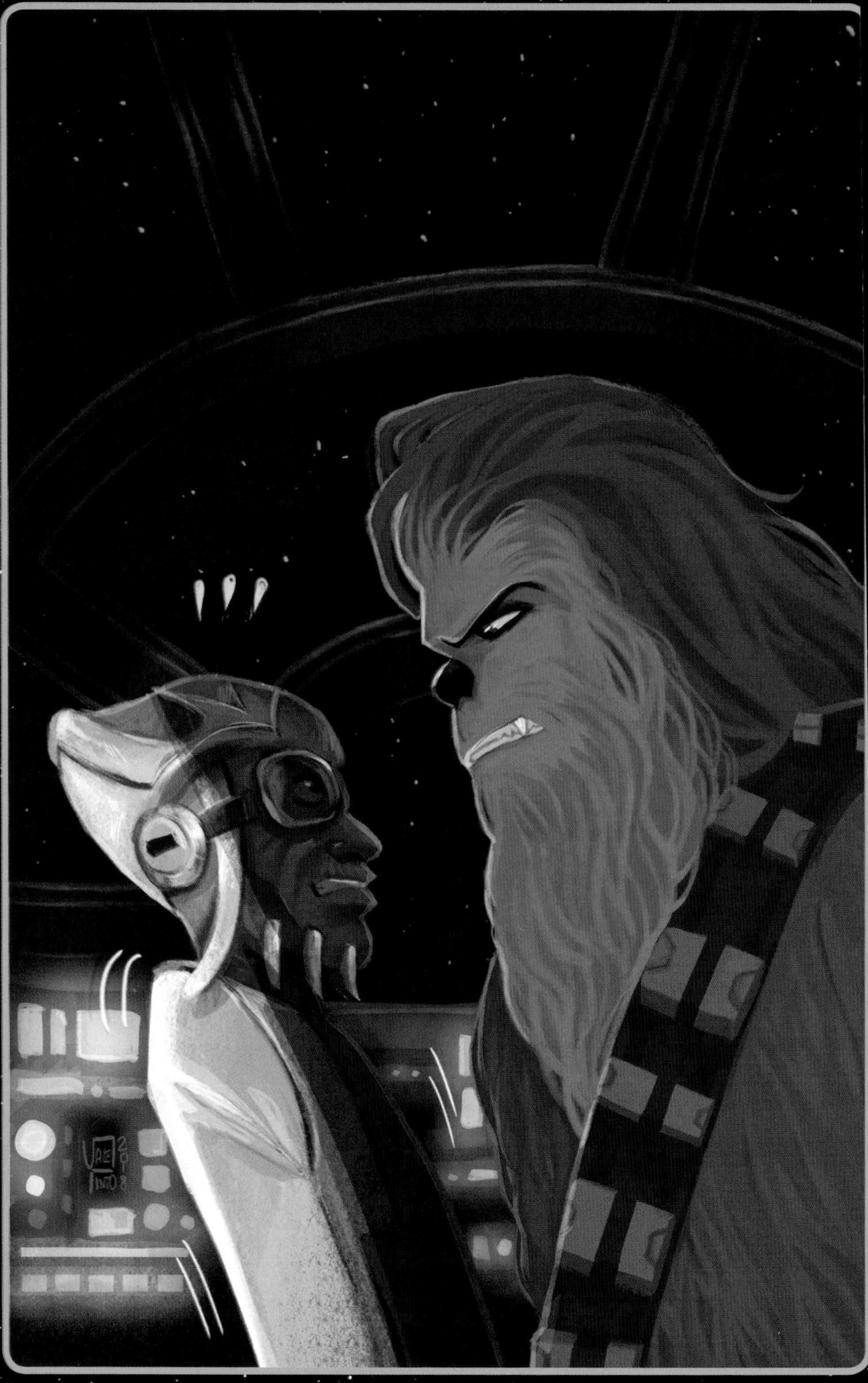

Art by Valentina Pinto

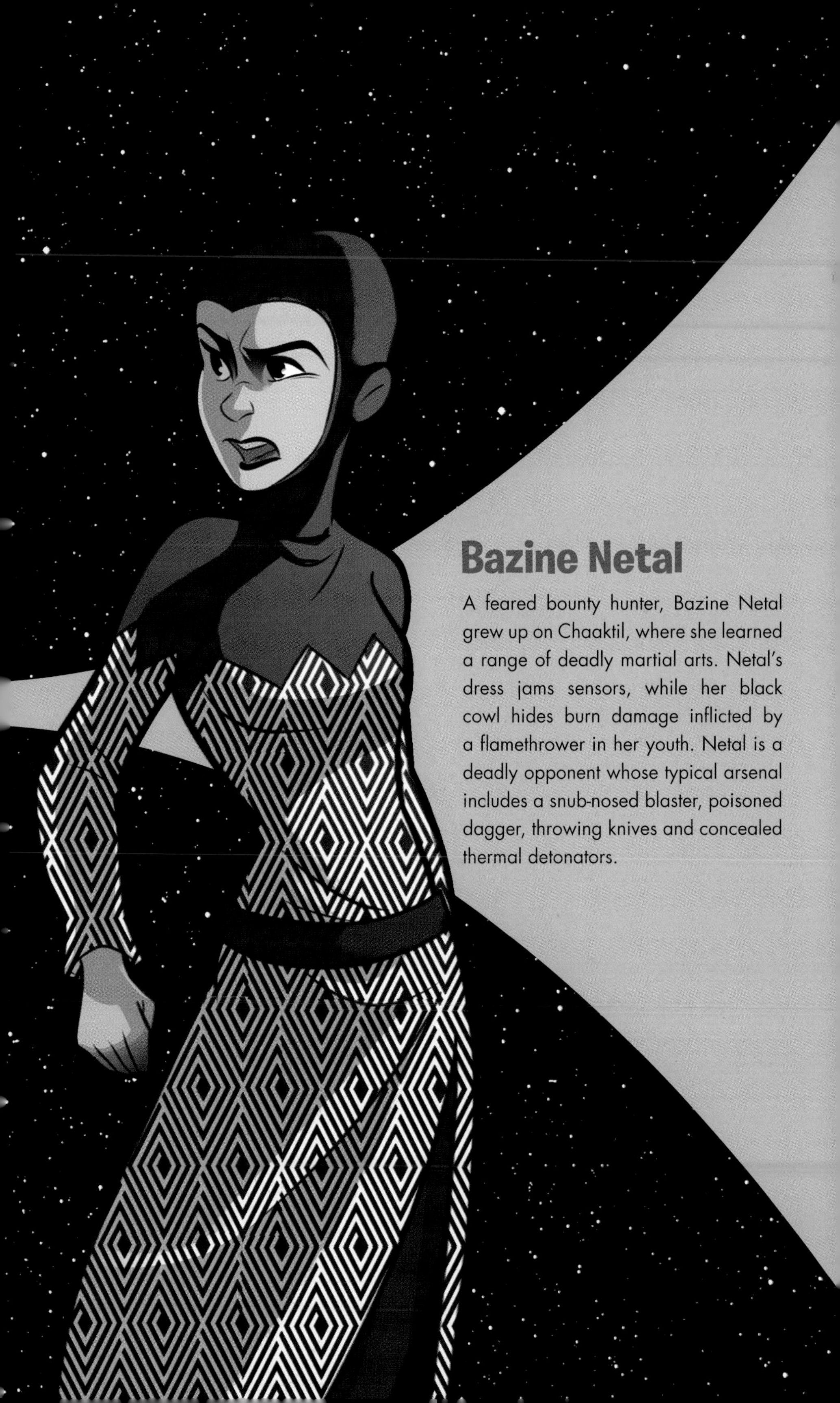

Bazine Netal

A feared bounty hunter, Bazine Netal grew up on Chaaktil, where she learned a range of deadly martial arts. Netal's dress jams sensors, while her black cowl hides burn damage inflicted by a flamethrower in her youth. Netal is a deadly opponent whose typical arsenal includes a snub-nosed blaster, poisoned dagger, throwing knives and concealed thermal detonators.

Embo

A fearsome bounty hunter of few words, Embo was quick to disable his target, be it by a single shot from his bowcaster or a decisive blow from his pan-shaped hat, which could be hurled at an adversary with deadly accuracy. The hat also doubled as a shield when the Kyuzo directly charged his target head first. A freelance hunter, Embo worked with the likes of Sugi and Boba Fett, loyal only to his faithful anooba, Marrok.

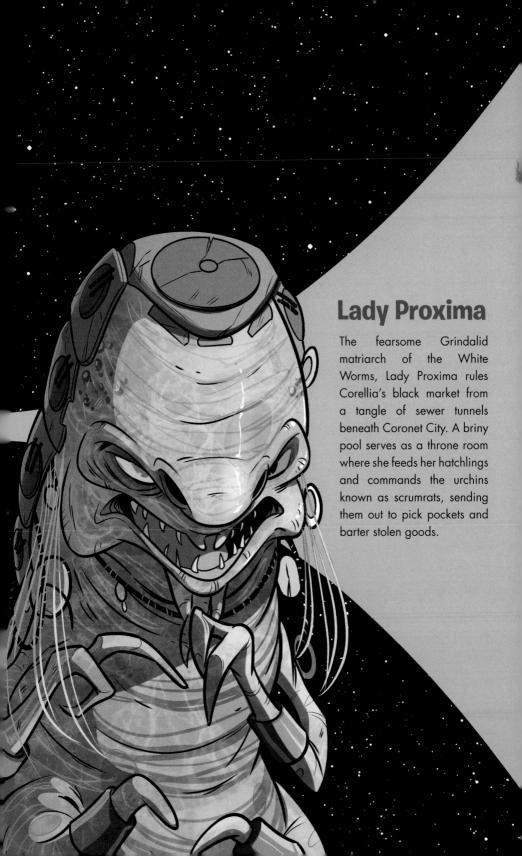

Lady Proxima

The fearsome Grindalid matriarch of the White Worms, Lady Proxima rules Corellia's black market from a tangle of sewer tunnels beneath Coronet City. A briny pool serves as a throne room where she feeds her hatchlings and commands the urchins known as scrumrats, sending them out to pick pockets and barter stolen goods.

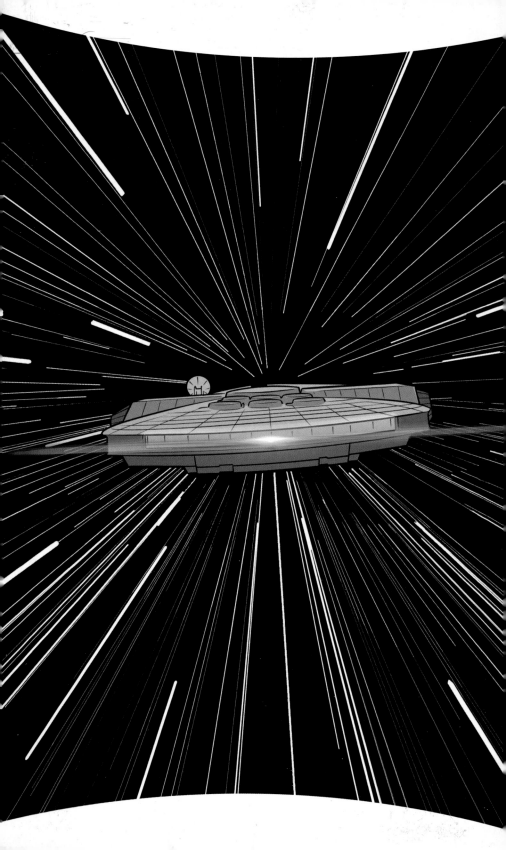